D1389427

LILLIA'S DIARY

The body of a beautiful young Estonian woman is found in a lake in rural Lancashire. Is it murder or a tragic accident? As Inspector Steve Carmichael begins to look into the dead woman's life, he discovers a wealth of secrets and embarks on a murder enquiry. Lillia Monroe was a woman who had expensive tastes and apparently had the money to satisfy them. Who did she meet regularly at a local hotel? How did she finance her love of things? And what does her diary reveal about her liaisons and her true feelings about the men in her life?

LILLIA'S DIARY

LILLIA'S DIARY

by

Ian McFadyen

Magna Large Print Books
Long Preston, North Yorkshire,
BD23 4ND, England.

British Library Cataloguing in Publication Data.

McFadyen, Ian
　　Lillia's diary.

A catalogue record of this book is
available from the British Library

ISBN　978-0-7505-3861-9

First published in Great Britain in 2009 by The Book Guild Ltd.

Published in Large Print 2014 by arrangement with
Book Guild Publishing

Magna Large Print is an imprint of Library Magna Books Ltd.

Printed and bound in Great Britain by
T.J. (International) Ltd., Cornwall, PL28 8RW

All characters in this publication are
fictitious and any resemblance to
real people, alive or dead,
is purely coincidental.

This book is dedicated to Alex Carvin,
a fine young man who was taken too soon.

Chapter 1

Lillia Monroe strode confidently into the hotel lobby. Upon her arrival at the reception desk, she smiled broadly.

'I'd like to check in,' she announced. 'The booking is in my husband's name as usual, John Burton.'

'Good afternoon, Mrs Burton,' replied an immaculately dressed young man behind the counter. 'I have you booked into your usual superior room, number 36.' The receptionist handed over the key to his guest, as he had done every Wednesday evening for the last twelve months.

Once Lillia was safely inside room 36 she flicked open her mobile phone and keyed in the numbers that she knew so well. 'I'm in the room, I'll see you later,' she softly whispered. 'Don't keep me waiting too long.'

Chapter 2

It had been a little over two years since the Carmichael family had arrived in Moulton Bank. After the trauma of those first few weeks, the family had all settled well into rural life. Penny had taken on part-time work in the village primary school, helping out in the office and occasionally supporting the teachers in IT lessons. Although it paid very little, the job fitted in nicely with family life and she found it stimulating to interface with other adults on a regular basis.

Jemma had just finished her A levels and was hoping her grades would be good enough to take her to university in Leeds. Her romance with Jason had evaporated some months earlier, much to the delight of her father. Although Jemma and Jason still remained on friendly terms, the truth was that she had become bored of him and, when the attraction of further education and life away from Moulton Bank started to beckon, she decided that she did not want to be tied into a relationship at home. She fully intended to enjoy all aspects of life at university.

Her brother Robbie was now sixteen and was enjoying a long break now his GCSEs were over. He had recently found himself a summer job at the local supermarket and was experiencing for the first time the freedom of purchasing CDs, DVDs and computer games without having to ask his parents for money. Unlike his elder sister, Robbie was not looking forward to his exam results. Although he was reasonably bright, he knew that he had not spent enough time studying and he was convinced that his grades would not be that brilliant.

Natalie, now eleven years old, had just finished at the local primary school and was looking forward to attending The West Lancashire School for Girls in September. After much pestering she had recently managed to persuade her parents to let her have a pony, which she had named Lucy and which was now the recipient of pretty much all of her spare time.

With the exception of his first month in the north, Steve had found work in the Lancashire CID pretty dull. The lack of any significant cases often made him yearn to return to London. He knew, though, that such a move would not be practical, as the family now felt very involved in village life. And although he was often bored at work, he did like living in Moulton Bank. He particularly enjoyed feeling part of a community, something he had never really experienced before and something that he now realised was sadly lacking in the impersonal world within the M25. And with less noise and much less traffic, he accepted, albeit reluctantly, that on balance the quiet country life did have some considerable advantages over life in a big city, and that his less challenging workload was just something he would have to live with.

'Jemma, are you out of that bathroom yet?' Steve bellowed up the stairs. 'We are going to be late for church.'

'We've still got plenty of time,' Penny replied calmly. 'There's nearly an hour before the service starts.'

'But I need a shave and she's been in there for at least half an hour already,' responded Steve angrily.

Penny shook her head and continued stacking the dishes in the dishwasher.

'I'm out now,' yelled Jemma.

Since the Reverend Pugh had retired, there had been a procession of clerics temporarily managing affairs in the parish. On this particular Sunday it was the Reverend George Feeney, the bumbling retired vicar of Newbridge, who graced the congregation by leading the service. Due to his work rota, Robbie was unable to join his parents and sisters at church that Sunday, much to his delight and the annoyance of his elder sister.

'This is so boring,' muttered Jemma to her mother as they knelt together in supposedly silent prayer.

'Not so loud,' replied Penny. 'Just think, in a few more weeks, if your results are good, you will be in Leeds so you won't have to come to church with us every Sunday.'

'Oh God,' whispered Jemma, 'please let me get straight As!'

For the next forty minutes the Reverend Feeney muddled through the service. Jemma remained silent, electing to amuse herself by texting her friends on her mobile. She had the common sense to set the mobile on silent and she carefully tried to hide her actions by discreetly holding the phone on the opposite side to her mother.

'Before you all depart,' announced the vicar at the end of the service, 'I have some good news. As from two weeks today, Moulton Bank will have a permanent vicar. Unfortunately I have foolishly left his details at home, but you will be pleased to know that he is a young chap and I'm sure he will make a splendid village pastor.'

'That's good, isn't it?' said Penny.

'Absolutely,' replied Steve. 'I don't think any of us can take any more services like this one!'

As was customary in the Carmichael weekly routine, the following Saturday lunchtime saw Steve and Penny pay a visit to the Railway Tavern for a few drinks. It was here that they first encountered their new village vicar.

'Please allow me to introduce you to Reverend Barnaby Green,' announced the landlord Robbie Robertson, as he pointed with great ceremony towards a very young, casually dressed man at the end of the bar.

'Reverend Green,' whispered Steve. 'Isn't he one of the suspects from Cluedo?'

'Yes, I'm afraid that's correct,' replied the young cleric with a grin. 'But it's a brilliant ice-breaker, don't you think?'

Steve had not realised his remark was said so loudly, and was relieved that it had not been taken badly by the new vicar. 'Pleased to meet you, vicar,' he said nervously. 'My name's Steve Carmichael and this is my wife,

Penny. Please let me buy you a drink.'

'Thank you,' he replied. 'Please call me Barney. I'll have another pint of lager.'

As soon as their drinks had arrived they made their way to a vacant table and sat down.

'That barmaid of yours is a real babe,' announced Barney to a shocked Robbie Robertson. 'Is she spoken for?'

'That's Katie,' responded Penny, trying hard to interrupt any further comments from the vicar. 'She's Robbie's daughter.'

'Is she really?' commented the vicar, who showed no sign of being embarrassed at all. 'I must say, Robbie, she's a lovely looking girl.' He then looked the landlord up and down and, with a broad smile, said, 'I suppose she must take after her mother.'

Robbie roared with laughter. 'Yes, she does take after her mum,' he replied. 'And she is single, but I warn you, I'll have no qualms about standing up for her if you take liberties, vicar or not.'

In the days that had passed since Reverend Feeney's announcement, Steve had wondered what the new cleric would be like, but he had never considered that their first meeting would be in the tap-room of the Railway Tavern. And he had certainly not expected him to be in his twenties and to be so completely un-vicar-like.

'I can see that I'm not exactly what you expected, am I?' enquired the vicar.

'Well, to be honest, vicar,' replied Steve carefully, 'although we've only just met, I can confidently say that you're nothing like I expected.'

'I understand,' responded Barney with a grin. 'I do tend to create an impression when people find out I'm a vicar.'

'I can well believe that,' said Steve.

Chapter 3

Loyalty and trust at work meant a great deal to Carmichael. He had spent a lot of time and energy over the past two years making sure that his subordinates understood exactly what he required from them in that respect. In return for their allegiance and support, Carmichael took every opportunity to help his officers develop their careers. Under his guidance the dependable Cooper had been promoted to sergeant and his other protégé, Marc Watson, was now, in

Steve's view, a much more focussed and committed officer than the person he had met two years earlier. Although Carmichael would be the first to admit that there was still plenty of room for more improvement, he took pride in the fact that Watson now stood a real chance of becoming an Inspector. This was something that Steve would have considered a million to one shot when he first arrived at the station.

In addition to the support that he could call upon from his two trusty lieutenants, Steve could also now rely on a number of young DCs, many of whom he also saw as promotion candidates. One in particular was Rachel Dalton, a local girl from one of the area's prominent dynasties. From an early age Rachel had been keen to join the police and since she had arrived, she had made it clear to all, including Steve, that she wanted to forge a career for herself without the assistance of her family's wealth or influence within the local community, which was not insignificant. Steve found that an admirable trait and he had a high regard for Rachel. Although Marc Watson would endlessly tease her about her background and her 'silver spoon' upbringing, even he had to admit that she was a capable officer and worthy of her place in Steve's team.

'How was your weekend?' Watson asked the young DC as he entered the office. 'Let me guess. I would say that you did a spot of grouse shooting and then had a few friends around for croquet on the lawn.'

Rachel was used to Marc's Monday morning greeting and remained calm. 'Actually, as you asked, I spent Saturday with some old school friends shopping in Manchester and yesterday I went to look at a few flats in Moulton Bank.'

'So the grouse had a peaceful weekend then?' Marc continued with a grin in the direction of some of the male DCs behind their desks.

'I'm impressed that you know that the grouse shooting season started on Sunday,' countered Rachel. A fact she somehow knew was true even though neither she nor anyone else in her family had ever fired a gun in their lives.

Paul Cooper peered over the huge pile of statements on his desk. 'Has anyone seen the boss?' he asked.

'Yes,' said Rachel. 'He's with Chief Inspector Hewitt.'

Steve had arrived well before any of the

other officers that morning and was now giving his superior a status report on current cases.

'So, the most pressing matters appear to be the recent spate of burglaries in some of the outlying villages, and the increase in alcohol-induced anti-social behaviour by a group of yobbos in Newbridge,' commented Hewitt.

'That's correct, sir,' said Steve, who was yearning for something more exciting to get his teeth into.

'But so far we have not had any reports of any break-ins yesterday?' said Hewitt.

'Not yet,' replied Steve.

'And all five so far were at houses where the owners were away and always during daylight hours on a Sunday,' continued Hewitt.

'That's right,' replied Steve. 'Our theory is that it's a day this person is always not working.'

Hewitt thought for a moment. 'These are just the sort of incidents that the Community Police should be resolving,' he said. 'I'll get them to step up their activities on the streets in the areas that have already had burglaries.'

Unlike Hewitt, Steve was not a great believer in the Community Police, he felt that they were neither one thing nor another.

'I'm not sure I agree,' he said. 'Surely these sorts of incidents would be more effectively handled by the regular uniformed officers? If we could get them more active, maybe with the support of the Community Police, then I think that would be the best way forward.'

Hewitt shook his head. 'I don't agree,' he said sharply. 'These are exactly the sort of crimes that Community Police were brought in to focus on. As you know, I was a strong advocate for us bolstering our resources by employing more men and women as Community Police Officers and I am convinced that they are the answer to reducing these sorts of crimes within our jurisdiction.'

Steve knew that he was not going to get his boss to budge on this issue and wisely elected not to argue the point any further.

It was after 9:30 am when Steve arrived back in the main CID suite. He briefed Cooper and Watson on the team's plans for the day, and then called Penny.

'I can't take any more of this mundane tedium,' he moaned down the phone. 'What I would give right now for an armed robbery or a suspicious death to look into.'

'I don't know why you can't just enjoy a

bit of peace and quiet,' replied Penny. 'I bet Marc Watson and Paul Cooper aren't sitting there hoping that some poor soul is murdered just so their adrenalin levels can get a boost.'

'Yes, but they are local lads,' snapped Steve, 'they are used to being bored.'

'Look, I'm going to have to go,' said Penny, who had no sympathy at all for her husband. 'I've a hair appointment in twenty minutes and I'm not ready.'

'OK,' replied Steve gloomily. 'I'll see you this evening.'

Chapter 4

Samantha Crouch had been working as a stylist in Helen Parke's salon for about eighteen months. She was a likable person and a first-class stylist, and without question was the main reason why the salon had seen a marked increase in business over the last year. Sam, as she preferred to be called, was very attractive, always well groomed, and was unattached. She was in her late twenties, outgoing and confident, and had become well known to most of the villagers of Moulton Bank. She was popular with her clients and had turned many a man's head in the village since she arrived. In fact there was really only one person in the village who was not a fan of Sam Crouch. Ever since they first met, Katie Robertson could only see the new stylist as a potential threat to her own, previously unchallenged position of village pin-up. Although there had been no open hostilities, it was evident to all that there was a degree of rivalry between these two ladies.

'Have you met the new vicar, Mrs Carmichael?' Sam asked almost as soon as Penny had sat down in the salon chair.

'Yes I have,' replied Penny. 'He's very different, isn't he?'

'Drop-dead gorgeous, I'd say,' continued Sam. 'Do you know if he's single?'

'I think so,' said Penny, remembering the way he was eyeing up Katie Robertson a few days earlier.

'Mind you, not being a church-goer, I think he's probably out of bounds to me,' continued Sam. 'I'm not sure vicars date atheists.'

Penny laughed. 'I don't know about that. They do say that opposites attract. Maybe he can convert you.'

'Or maybe me him,' Sam replied with a mischievous smile.

At that moment the salon door opened and in walked Hannah De Vere.

'Please take a seat, Mrs De Vere,' Sam said in a way that suggested the salon's next client was an important customer. 'Helen's just popped out to the bank. She'll be back in a few minutes. Sophie,' Sam said to the young, bored trainee who was propping herself up at the far end of the salon, 'can you get Mrs De Vere some refreshments while she's waiting for Helen?' Sophie shuffled clumsily across the salon floor to the now seated VIP.

'Would you like tea or coffee?' she asked in a tone that suggested she did not share Sam's perception of Mrs De Vere's status.

'No I'm fine, Sophie dear,' replied Mrs De Vere with a gentle smile. The expressionless trainee made a 180 degree turn and shuffled back to her original place at the end of the salon. She did not notice the exasperated look that Sam gave Penny in the mirror.

'How are you, Hannah?' Penny said.

'Oh, Penny, I didn't see you there,' said Mrs De Vere with genuine surprise. 'I'm absolutely fine.'

Penny had known Hannah Bolton since

they were small children. There was only a few days' difference in their ages, and their mothers, who had met in hospital when the girls were born, had remained friends for pretty much the entire time the girls had been living at home. Hannah's parents had been employed by Henry De Vere, who in those days was a man in his late seventies. Hannah's father was in charge of De Vere's horses, while her mother was the family cook. Although Penny and Hannah had grown up together and went to the same schools they had mixed in different company. Penny was more gregarious and spent more time in her younger days in the company of boys, while Hannah was more shy and had led an altogether more quiet existence, preferring to spend her spare time helping her father with the horses. It had therefore been a huge shock to the entire community when Hannah Bolton, at the age of only nineteen became engaged to Charles De Vere, the only son and heir of Henry De Vere, and a man some fifteen years her senior.

'Young Natalie is doing really well with that pony you bought her,' said Hannah with a smile. 'She's a natural.'

'She's obsessed with it,' replied Penny. 'It's

all she talks about and I'm sure it's all she thinks about too.'

'I didn't know your daughter had a pony,' Sam said, trying hard to join in the conversation.

'Yes,' replied Penny. 'She had been pestering Steve and me for years to get her one, but until I mentioned it to Hannah, we didn't see how we could. But Hannah was really kind and has allowed us to buy one of their ponies for her and has agreed to keep her stabled at the manor.'

'It was no problem for us,' interjected Hannah. 'We are pleased to help out and, to be honest, Natalie is a fantastic help to us with Lucy and the other horses.'

'So that was the deal then?' enquired Sam. 'Natalie works at the stables to pay for the horse's keep?'

'Pretty much,' replied Penny. 'So it's a good deal for us, that's for sure.'

'And for us. You see, we've only six horses and ponies at home now,' said Hannah. 'When my father retired last year we decided that it was not practical to employ someone specifically to manage them any more, but it's still too much for Charles and me to manage alone with all our other commitments. So we decided to sell a couple of the ponies on the condition that the owners retained them at the manor and that they would help out with all the horses at weekends and in the school holidays.'

'Sounds a good deal all round then,' said Sam as she finished Penny's hair. 'So, do you not have plans to buy more horses?'

'No,' replied Hannah sadly. 'Alas, Charles is not as keen on horses as I am or was his father. At one time his father had about twenty or thirty at the stable, and also had some that he raced. But those days have gone. Charles is much more interested in greyhound racing than he is in horses, I'm afraid.'

'I didn't know that,' Penny said with some astonishment in her voice. 'Of course, I knew you were no longer involved in horse racing, but I had no idea you were keen on greyhound racing.'

'Oh yes,' said Hannah. 'Charles has about six with Stan Foster, who races them at the White City stadium near Blackpool.'

'How thrilling,' said Penny. 'I've never seen greyhound racing. Do you have many winners?'

'Yes we do,' said Hannah. 'We go to watch them regularly, why don't you join us sometime?'

'We'd really enjoy that,' replied Penny excitedly.

Penny checked her hair in the mirror, nodded positively at Sam and made her way to the reception desk to pay.

'Actually, we are going this Thursday evening,' said Hannah as she sat down ready for her hair to be washed. 'We have a runner so why don't you and Steve join us?'

'That would be great,' replied Penny. 'I'll check with Steve but I'm sure it will be fine. I'll call you tomorrow to confirm.'

Penny paid for her hair and made her next appointment for six weeks' time. She gave Sam a £5 tip, which was her customary tip for the stylist, and left a £2 tip for Sophie, who, to Penny's delight, had managed to wash her hair this time without either soaking her back or scalding her scalp.

'I'll phone you tomorrow, Hannah,' she said as she made her exit. 'And should I look forward to seeing a little more of you at church from now on?' she whispered to Sam.

'You never know,' replied Sam with a glint in her eye. 'I may just surprise you.'

Chapter 5

It was a warm summer morning with not a cloud in sight. Only the faint traces of aircraft engine vapours punctuated the faultless blue canopy. All was silent, save only for the gentle lapping of the waves or the occasional cry of a far-off bird. The teenage boy lay back in the boat and looked up into the sky. He let his hand slip into the cool clear water and slowly moved it around in small regular circles.

Suddenly his fingers became entwined in what he thought were weeds or maybe a disregarded fishing net. As his hand explored the long strands he discovered that they were either wrapped around or more likely, attached to something hard and round. He slowly peered over the side of the boat to see the pale white face of a woman staring back up at him, her eyes fixed with the cold expression of fear.

When Carmichael arrived at the lake, Cooper and Watson were already on the scene.

'What do we have?' Steve asked.

'A woman in her mid to late twenties, well dressed, good-looking, but with no ID,' replied Watson. 'She was found by that young boy over there, when he was out fishing in that small rowing boat.' Watson pointed further down the bank where a boy in his late teens was sitting next to a tatty old wooden boat. The boy was clearly shocked by what he had found, so Steve was pleased to see that the young man was already being attended to by Rachel Dalton, who was crouched down next to him with her hand on his arm to provide a degree of comfort. Steve then looked down at the small limp torso that had been carefully laid out on her back. Although he'd seen many dead bodies in the course of his career, Carmichael always felt the same when he saw a new murder victim. This was someone's daughter, he thought. She's probably also someone's dear little sister, maybe a loving wife or girlfriend and possibly and most saddening of all, some young child's mother.

'Do we have any idea of how long the body has been in the water, or how she died?' Steve asked.

'I asked the forensic people but they would not commit themselves on what they thought was the cause of death,' responded

Cooper. 'However, one of them did say that, looking at the state of the body, he thought that she'd been in there for at least a few days, but no more than a week.'

'You're right, Marc,' Steve said quietly. 'She was indeed a good-looking girl.'

As a rule, Carmichael avoided attending autopsies. On this occasion he felt compelled to be present. With no ID for the body yet, he was keen to gain as much information as he could about the young woman and how she came to be in the lake.

Since his arrival in Moulton Bank he had built up a high regard for Dr Stock, who he considered to be one of the most professional pathologists he had ever worked with. What Steve admired most about Stock was his ability to quickly piece together the evidence to help the police understand not only the circumstances of the death, but also gain an insight into the persona of the perpetrator, a trait he had not come across before in a pathologist. Stock was never vague, nor did he jump to wild conclusions. If he was sure of something he would say so and, if there was an element of doubt he would make sure that this was clear too.

Carmichael and Watson stood a few paces

back as the pathologist started the autopsy. The woman's figure suggested that she took great care of herself when she was alive. Her finger-nails and toe-nails were all neatly tended, and it struck Steve that, with her looks and figure, she probably had a career that valued her considerable natural attributes.

Suddenly Steve's mobile rang, much to the disgust of the pathologist, who had already started to dictate into his small recording machine.

'Sorry, Stock, I thought I'd switched it off,' he apologised as he looked at the incoming number. 'I'll take this outside.'

A few minutes later Steve re-entered the room. 'Sorry, gentlemen, but I need to go. Cooper thinks he may have come up with an identity for our young lady,' he announced excitedly.

'Great news,' said Watson, who was relieved that this might mean him being excused the sight of Stock's gruesome investigations. 'Where is he?'

'He's in Little Oakley,' replied Carmichael. 'But I need you to stay here with Dr Stock. Cooper and I can manage. Call me as soon as you find anything interesting.'

Stock smiled to himself. He had yet to find

a policeman who had the stomach for an autopsy.

'If the person he's found is born and bred and lived all her life in England, she's unlikely to be your lady, Steve,' announced the pathologist as he continued to examine the young woman.

'Why do you say that?' asked Steve in amazement.

'Her dental work is unusual. I'd need to do some more research but it's not the sort of work I'd expect from a dentist in the UK,' replied Stock. 'I would guess it's from a good dentist, but probably one that practises in Scandinavia, Germany or maybe Eastern Europe.'

Steve smiled, shook his head in disbelief and made his way to the car park.

As usual it looked like Stock's autopsy report was going to be invaluable to the investigation.

Chapter 6

Gemini Technologies was located in a small industrial estate on the outskirts of Little Oakley, a small village about five miles from Moulton Bank. As Carmichael pulled into the complex he could see Cooper's battered blue Rover occupying the only space in the company's visitors car park.

'So, what's the score?' Steve asked.

'We took a call this morning from a Mrs Andrews at Gemini,' replied Cooper. 'She was worried because one of her colleagues, a Lillia Monroe, had not been in work for the last two days and there had been no answer on her mobile. She emailed over a scanned picture that she had of the missing woman and, although it's not that good a picture, it looks like it's the body from the lake.' With that Cooper showed Carmichael the photograph.

Carmichael studied carefully the picture of a stunning young woman in a low-cut red evening dress, wearing an unusual but slightly distorted diamond encrusted cross, smiling broadly into the camera.

'There's no doubt at all,' remarked Carmichael. 'Our lady is Lillia Monroe.'The two policemen made their way into the small reception area and asked the receptionist if they could see Mrs Andrews.Within a matter of minutes a woman in her early forties arrived and introduced herself as Ruth Andrews, PA to the managing director. The policemen showed her their identity cards and followed her through the main door into an open plan office area.

It was clear that the whole office was aware of who the visitors were and why they had come. As Carmichael and Cooper walked through into one of only three small offices, they could feel the attention of dozens of pairs of eyes and could hear mutterings from the neatly organised workers in their comfortable partitioned workstations.

'I do hope she's all right,' Ruth Andrews remarked as they closed the door.

'I'm afraid we may have bad news,' replied Carmichael. 'A woman who very closely resembles the photograph you sent to the station was found dead earlier today.'

Ruth Andrews slumped down into a chair and put her hand over her mouth.

'I know that this must be a great shock to

you, but can you tell me where she lived and if she had any relatives?' continued Carmichael.

'Yes, of course,' said Ruth. 'She lives in Station Mews with her husband.'

'Husband!' exclaimed Carmichael. 'So what is he saying about her being missing?'

'We weren't able to contact him either,' replied Ruth. 'We believe that he's abroad on business.'

'Oh dear,' replied Carmichael.

'I went to their house yesterday evening,' continued Ruth. 'I was very worried. It was empty and although the curtains were open it did not look like anyone had been there for a while.'

'Why do you say that?' asked Cooper.

'Well, I could see that there were at least three newspapers in the porch,' continued Ruth. 'They have a glass porch so it's quite easy to see in.'

'I see,' replied Carmichael. 'Can you tell me what Mrs Monroe did here?'

'Well,' said Ruth hesitantly, 'she had been with us about two years and although she started on the sales desk, she had done really well for herself and was now our Communications Manager.'

'What does a Communications Manager

do?' probed Carmichael.

'Well, she would sort out our PR, put together advertising campaigns and manage exhibitions for the company,' replied Ruth.

'I see,' said Steve for a second time. 'I'd like to see her office and can you please get me Mrs Monroe's home address and her telephone number?'

'Of course,' replied Ruth, who gently got up out of the chair and walked over to the door. 'Do you think there is any chance that the woman you have is not Lillia?' she asked as she reached the door.

'It's possible,' replied Steve. 'We will need to have some formal identification, but I'm afraid the likeness between the body we have found and your photograph is very strong.'

On hearing this news, Ruth Andrews' head tilted forward and she gazed down at Carmichael's shoes.

'If you would care to follow me, gentlemen,' she said quietly. 'Lillia's office is upstairs.' Carmichael and Cooper followed Mrs Andrews out of the office and up a short flight of stairs. At the top of the landing were four doors. One was open and was clearly the company's boardroom. The others were all shut. On each of these doors were nameplates.

'Ralf Marsh, Tom Sharwood and Lillia Monroe,' Carmichael read out loud. 'Who are the two gentlemen?'

'Mr Marsh is the Managing Director,' replied Ruth. 'And Mr Sharwood is our Financial Controller. I'm afraid they are both out today.' Ruth Andrews led Carmichael and Cooper into Lillia Monroe's office.

'I'll get you that information,' she said as she left the office.

The first thing that struck Steve when he looked around the office was that here was a woman with expensive tastes. The furniture all looked luxurious and new. Her walls had framed, original paintings and in the corner of the room was a music system that looked as though it had cost a fortune. However it was the large gilt-framed photograph of Lillia that stood on her desk that grabbed Steve's attention.

'This is the original of the one that Mrs Andrews sent you,' Steve remarked. 'It's a great photo, but it's slightly strange for someone to have a photo of themselves on their desk, don't you think?'

'I suppose it is,' replied Cooper. 'Maybe it has some happy memory attached to it.'

'Maybe,' whispered Carmichael as he picked it up.

'She was a real looker wasn't she?' observed Cooper.

'Yes,' replied Steve. 'I bet she was not short of admirers.'

At that juncture the door opened and Ruth Andrews returned. In her hand she held a small piece of paper. 'This is Lillia's address and her home and mobile numbers. I've also included the details of her company car,' she said as she handed the paper to Cooper.

'Mrs Monroe had a company car?' Steve asked.

'Yes,' replied Ruth.

'And I suppose it's a bright coloured convertible,' he continued.

'Yes, it's red. Have you found it?'

Steve smiled. Although he had never met Lillia Monroe when she was alive, he was starting to feel that he knew her quite well.

'No,' he said with a wry smile, 'it was just a guess.'

'What happens now?' asked Mrs Andrews.

'Well, we will need someone to identify the body,' replied Cooper. 'But that should really be her husband. Do you know where he works or how we might contact him?'

Mrs Andrews shook her head. 'I don't, I'm afraid. I think he works in the electronics industry, a Sales Manager, I think. I'm sure

Tom would know as they play rugby together at Newbridge Rugby Club.'

'It would be helpful if you could get me Mr Sharwood's mobile number before we go,' Carmichael said, 'and that of the Managing Director too.'

'Of course,' replied Mrs Andrews.

'We will also need to take statements from those in the office who were close to her,' added Cooper.

'Well, to be honest,' replied Mrs Andrews hesitantly, 'I can't think of anyone that works here who was really that close to her. I don't want to speak ill of the dead, but she wasn't that popular with the staff here. I can't speak for Mr Marsh or Mr Sharwood but the rest of the people here were not close to her at all.'

'Do you think they resented her rapid rise from the sales office to Communications Manager?' Cooper asked.

'I think that was probably part of it,' replied Mrs Andrews. 'Mind you, they didn't like her much when she was on the sales desk. She didn't really try to mix with any of them and, as a matter of fact they were surprised that Mr Marsh had not let her go. As far as I know, her sales figures were pretty poor when she did that job, and people who don't perform normally don't last long here.'

'Is that right?' enquired Carmichael. 'But was she good at her new role?'

'Yes, I think Mr Marsh was happy with her work,' said Mrs Andrews. 'But I know Mr Sharwood was concerned that our advertising and promotional costs had gone through the roof in the last year.'

'We'd like to spend some time alone here, if we may, Mrs Andrews,' continued Carmichael. 'Can you get us those telephone numbers?'

'Of course,' she responded. 'I'll leave you in peace.'

'Oh, before you go,' continued Carmichael, 'was Lillia originally from outside the country?'

'Yes, she was,' replied Mrs Andrews with astonishment. 'She was from Estonia.'

Carmichael smiled, Dr Stock had done it again, he thought.

After Mrs Andrews had departed, Carmichael and Cooper spent a few minutes looking through the contents of Lillia Monroe's desk drawers and filing cabinet. In truth they yielded nothing new to help the investigation.

'So, what do you think, sir?' asked Cooper.

'Not sure,' replied Carmichael. 'She was clearly a woman who liked the finer things in life and all this and her car point to her being very conscious of her status. However, other than that, there's not much to go on.'

'Do you think she used her looks and charm to get all this?' Cooper asked with his arms stretched out.

'We should not jump to conclusions, but it's a definite maybe,' replied Carmichael. 'We need to talk with her husband, though, and also to Marsh and Sharwood. I'm sure once we have done that we will have a better idea of the sort of person she was and maybe some clues to why she ended up in the lake.'

Before they left the office Steve took the picture of Lillia from her desk. 'I don't think anyone will mind if we borrow this,' he said.

The two officers looked at the pretty smiling face in the photograph. 'That's an unusual necklace she is wearing,' remarked Cooper.

'Yes, I thought that,' replied Carmichael.

Around Lillia's neck was a striking gold and diamond cross, with smaller bars at right angles at the top of the cross and at the ends of the horizontal bar, and a fourth, longer bar mid-way down the centre shaft, which was angled at about 45 degrees.

'It's not your average Anglican's cross, is

it?' said Cooper. 'Do you want me to check it out?'

'No,' replied Steve. 'We can do that later if it seems important. You get the telephone numbers from Mrs Andrews and try and call Sharwood and Marsh. Also, see if you can get Mr Monroe's number from Sharwood and contact him too. I'll get back to see how Marc and Stock are getting on. Let's try and meet back at the station for a debrief at about six o'clock.'

'Right you are, sir.' replied Cooper.

'Ask Rachel to be there too,' continued Carmichael. 'I'd like to know what the boy who found her body had to say.'

Chapter 7

By the time Carmichael arrived back at the hospital mortuary it was already after three o'clock. Stock had concluded his post mortem and was with Watson in his small office discussing the results. As usual Stock's young assistant had been given the task of tidying up the room and making Lillia's body look as presentable as was possible, given the major

44

intrusive activity that had taken place.

'Perfect timing,' announced Stock cheerily, when he saw Steve arrive. 'Care for a coffee?'

Out of the corner of his eye, Steve could see that Marc was already drinking. He looked pale and clearly had not enjoyed witnessing the autopsy.

'Yes please,' replied Steve. 'Two sugars and just a drop of milk in mine.'

Stock made his way over to a small kettle, switched it on and started rummaging in a cabinet for another cup.

'So, what did you conclude?' asked Steve.

'She was a beautiful specimen of a woman,' replied Stock as he found a mug. 'I have put her age at between twenty-five and thirty. She was five feet ten inches tall, weighed 9st 8lbs and had not had any children.'

'And how did she die?' Steve asked.

'That is where it gets a bit tricky,' replied Stock as he poured the hot water from the kettle into Steve's mug. 'She drowned in the lake, is the answer, but there was a major bruise at the back of her head.'

'So do you think she was knocked out and then thrown into the lake?' Steve asked.

'That's possible, but another possibility is that she could have slipped backwards, banged her head, rendering herself unconscious, and then either fallen into the lake or was put there by someone,' replied Stock as he handed Steve the mug of coffee.

'But you would say her death is suspicious?' prompted Steve.

'Yes,' responded Stock. 'I would say that it was not suicide and the blow on the head did happen before she entered the water, so yes, I would say her death requires some explanation, as it could well have been caused by the actions of a person as yet unknown.'

Steve took a sip of coffee, but after discovering that it was not sugared, rested it on the table in front of him.

'When do you think she died?' he asked.

'Again, not possible to be exact, but I would guess that she had been in the water for over twenty-four hours, but certainly no more than two days,' replied Stock.

'So from Saturday morning at the earliest to Monday morning,' announced Marc, who was slowly recovering from the ordeal of the autopsy.

'Yes, I'd say that would be the time frame we are talking about. But, given that her last meal appears to have been toast and cereal my suggestion is that she was probably drowned after her breakfast but before lunch, on either Saturday or Sunday,' concluded Stock.

'Which do you think is more likely?' Steve asked, hoping that he may be able to narrow it down a bit further.

'I would really not like to say,' responded Stock. 'Judging by the state of the body it was more likely to be Sunday morning rather than Saturday. But that would be without hard evidence to support this. If it were Saturday I could probably accept that too.'

Steve removed the photograph that he had taken from Lillia's office and showed it to Stock. 'We are pretty sure that this is our body,' he said.

Stock looked closely at the picture. 'Yes, I think you're right,' he replied. 'And by the look of that necklace she is wearing, my theory that she was from Eastern Europe looks likely to be right.'

'Why do you say that?' Steve asked.

'Do you not know what it is?' Stock asked with a superior smirk.

'Actually no,' Steve replied.

'It's a Russian Orthodox Church symbol,' announced Stock with an air of triumph. 'I suspect there are not that many indigenous Brits who would wear such a necklace.'

'She was Russian then?' commented Marc.

'No, Lillia Monroe was from Estonia,' replied Steve, trying hard to appear as learned as the pathologist.

'Well, I don't know for sure,' continued Stock, 'but that would fit as I suspect that many Estonians are Russian Orthodox, given that Estonia was until very recently part of the Soviet Union.'

Steve nodded. 'Certainly there will be more Russian Orthodox people there than you would expect to find in Lancashire.'

Stock handed the photograph back to Steve. 'I'll type up the report this evening and get it to you in the morning,' he announced in a business-like way.

'Thanks,' replied Steve as he put the photograph back in his pocket.

Cooper had remained at Gemini in Lillia's office. As he waited for Mrs Andrews to return with the mobile numbers for Sharwood and Marsh, he started to look through some of the company literature on Lillia's desk. The brochures were all expensive-looking and glossy. As he leafed through, Cooper learned a bit more about Gemini's business. They appeared to be essentially a beauty products company, specialising in creams and oils which were promoted as anti-ageing products and sold under the company's slogan 'Natural Youthful Beauty'.

Mrs Andrews returned to the office with an A4 sheet of paper in her hand. 'I have the numbers for you, sergeant,' she said.

'Thank you,' replied Cooper. 'So, Gemini is a beauty products company?'

'We like to think that we are much more than that,' she replied sharply. 'Our market is mainly women over thirty who take a pride in their appearance and wish to slow down the effects of time on their skin.'

'And do these products work?' he asked.

'Absolutely,' replied Mrs Andrews passionately. 'I use them myself and would recommend them to anyone.'

Cooper could not help thinking that Mrs Andrews was probably not the best advert for the company's products, but was neither brave enough nor sufficiently rude to pass comment.

Mrs Andrews handed over the paper to Cooper. 'I know that Mr Marsh will not be contactable until this evening, as he's with a major client, and he always switches his phone off when he's with customers, but Mr Sharwood should be available. I had a conversation with him this morning before I called the station about Mrs Monroe and I've also spoken to him just now. He's playing golf today but he is expecting your call and says he will keep his phone on.'

'Thank you,' replied Cooper. 'I've just a few other requests if that's all right. Firstly can you get me the home addresses of Mr Marsh and Mr Sharwood and, finally, would it be possible for me to make the call from here?'

'Of course,' she responded. 'Just dial nine for an outside line.' With that Mrs Andrews left the office to fetch her managers' addresses, making sure she closed the door behind her.

The de-briefing commenced at six o'clock prompt. Steve started by updating the team on the conversation that he and Cooper had had with Ruth Andrews and giving a brief outline of the initial findings from the post-mortem.

'We should be careful not to jump to any conclusions until we have Stock's full report and we have a formal identification that the dead woman is Lillia Monroe,' he said. 'However, at this stage we should assume that the body will be identified as Lillia and that her death was caused as a result of suspicious circumstances.'

Watson, Cooper and Rachel Dalton all

nodded in agreement.

'So, Rachel, what did the boy who found the body have to say?' Carmichael asked.

'The boy is an eighteen-year-old called Michael Hornby,' replied Rachel. 'He had been out alone in the old boat, fishing since about six-thirty this morning. He says he was not having any luck fishing and was just lazing in the boat when he felt the body in the water.'

'What time was it when he found the body?' Carmichael asked.

'He did not have a watch but reckoned it would have been about nine o'clock, maybe nine-thirty,' replied Rachel. 'He says he phoned 999 pretty much straight away on his mobile and the call is recorded at nine-thirty-four.'

'So how did the body get on the bank?' asked Cooper. 'Surely he couldn't manage to get it out of the lake and to the shore himself?'

'No,' replied Rachel. 'He had a half-full four-litre bottle of water in the boat so he tipped it out and put the top back on, tied it to the dead woman's arm with some doubled up fishing line and used it as a float. That way he figured that the body would stay buoyant and would be easily located later. He then rowed back to the bank and waited for the police to arrive.'

'Sounds a smart lad,' Carmichael replied.

'Yes,' continued Rachel. 'He was really shaking when I spoke with him but his actions were amazing given what he had just found.'

Carmichael then turned to face Cooper. 'Did you manage to speak to Marsh and Sharwood, and most importantly, have you managed to locate Lillia's husband?' he asked.

'I've spoken to Sharwood,' replied Cooper. 'He gave me Bradley Monroe's mobile number. He confirmed that Mr Monroe is in Frankfurt on business and is not due back until Friday. I've tried to call him several times but it just goes through to voicemail.'

'What about Sharwood and Marsh?' Steve asked. 'What have they to say about all this?'

'Sharwood was very shocked and seemed really upset on the phone,' replied Cooper. 'He said that he would be in the office tomorrow and on Thursday if we needed to speak to him further. No luck with Marsh, though. He has had his phone on voicemail too, all afternoon.'

'OK,' said Steve calmly. 'We can't do much more this evening. We do need to track them both down, but particularly Bradley Monroe. If you give me his mobile number before you go I'll try calling him again this evening, you keep trying Marsh.'

'OK, sir,' replied Cooper.

'In the morning I'd like you two,' Steve said, pointing at Rachel and Cooper, 'to start looking for Lillia's car. I also want you to see if you can locate where she was put into the water.'

'Yes, sir,' replied Cooper.

'Marc,' continued Carmichael. 'You and I need to put our energies into finding Bradley Monroe and getting him back over here. If I can't speak with him this evening then we need to try to track him down through his work. Paul, did Sharwood give you the details of where he worked?'

'To be honest, I didn't ask,' replied Cooper sheepishly. 'Do you want me to call him back?'

'It can wait until the morning,' replied Carmichael, 'but if we can speak with Mr Monroe tonight that would be the best scenario.' Steve paused, looked around at his team and said, 'OK, let's call it a day. We need to get back together briefly tomorrow morning at eight-thirty for a five-minute update.' Cooper, Watson and Dalton all stood up to leave.

'Rachel, can you let me have the statements from Michael Hornby and the officers who were first at the scene? I'll read them later this evening,' said Carmichael. 'And Paul, I need the mobile number for Bradley Monroe before you go.'

Steve did not stay too long at the office that evening. He decided that he would take the three statements home to read. He also wanted to make the call to Bradley Monroe from his home office before it got too late. When he arrived home, Penny was waiting for him.

'Hello, darling,' she said as she gave him a kiss. 'Have you been involved with the body in the lake? I heard about it on the radio.'

'Yes,' replied Steve. 'It may actually just be an accidental death, but I have a feeling that it wasn't.' Steve pulled out the picture of Lillia from his pocket. 'This is the poor unfortunate lady. Well, we are pretty sure it is.'

'Poor girl,' replied Penny. 'That's an interesting necklace she's wearing.'

'Apparently it's a Russian Orthodox cross,' replied Steve. 'At least, that's what Stock says.'

'So was she a Russian call girl?' Penny asked.

Steve was shocked by his wife's question.

'Why do you say that?' he asked.

'Just the first thought that came into my mind when I saw the photo,' replied Penny, who was starting to feel embarrassed to have jumped to such a conclusion about a poor dead woman she had never met. 'She looks like a glamorous girl and if that cross is a Russian Orthodox cross I just assumed she was Russian.'

'To the best of our knowledge she was not involved as an escort or anything like that,' he said indignantly. 'She's actually Estonian. She had a good job in marketing and was married. She appears to have been a woman that men were attracted to, but, judging by your remarks, maybe not so popular with the ladies.'

'Do you want any tea?' said Penny, trying hard to change the subject.

'Yes, that would be great,' replied Steve. 'I just need half an hour in my study to read some statements and to make a few calls first.'

'OK,' replied Penny, who kissed him again. 'I'll sort you something out.'

Steve smiled and walked upstairs to his study.

Chapter 8

'Good morning, The Lindley Hotel and Spa,' said the receptionist, 'Sarah speaking, how can I help you?'

'I'd like to cancel my room for this evening,' announced the caller.

'Can I take your name please?' enquired the receptionist.

'Yes, it's Mr Burton,' he replied, 'John Burton.'

'Oh, hello,' replied the receptionist, who had got to know Mr Burton fairly well in the last twelve months. 'That's fine, it's all cancelled.'

'Thank you,' replied the caller.

'Will we be seeing you and Mrs Burton next week as usual?' she asked, mischievously.

'I'm not sure,' he replied. 'But if I need the room next week I'll call through my booking over the weekend, as I normally do.' Sarah Pennington smiled to herself. It was common knowledge at the hotel that Mr and Mrs Burton were not married, well at least, not to each other. However, nobody knew much about the suave gentleman who always made the booking and paid in cash, or his extremely attractive partner with the soft Eastern European accent.

'Maybe she's dumped him for someone richer,' Sarah thought.

Carmichael's team were all assembled in the briefing room at 8:30 as he had requested.

'Morning, team,' he said cheerily. 'Good news on Bradley Monroe. I spoke to him last night and he was getting the first flight back this morning from Frankfurt. It arrived in Manchester about ten minutes ago and I have arranged for Mr Monroe to be collected and brought straight to the hospital to make the formal identification.'

'Great news, boss,' replied Watson.

'I managed to make contact with Marsh as well last night,' said Cooper. 'He already knew about the body and our visit to the office yesterday. He said if there was anything he could do to help then we should let him know.'

'How did he know about us finding Lillia?' asked Steve.

'He said that he'd spoken with Mrs Andrews and that Tom Sharwood had also called him.'

'Figures, I guess,' said Carmichael. 'I suspect the first thing Ruth Andrews did when we left the office yesterday was to call both men.'

'So, what are our instructions for today, sir?' asked Rachel eagerly.

'As we discussed last night, I would like you and Cooper to look for the car and try and find the place where Lillia fell, or was put in the lake,' said Steve. 'But in view of the developments in finding the husband, Marc and I will need to spend today with him.'

'Do you still want us to follow up on Mr Monroe's place of work?' Cooper asked.

'Not now,' replied Steve. 'Maybe later if need be, but you just put your energies behind finding Lillia's car and how she got in the lake, and Marc and I will focus on Mr Monroe.'

'Yes, sir,' replied Cooper.

'We should all get back together again this afternoon,' said Steve, looking at his watch. 'Let's do it at three pm.'

'Sir,' said Rachel, 'I nearly forgot. Chief Inspector Hewitt asked to see you as soon as we had finished the briefing.'

Steve raised his eyes to the ceiling. 'OK.'

he said. 'Marc, you get yourself off to the mortuary to meet Mr Monroe. Call ahead to Stock to make sure the body is ready for the ID, but don't do it until I get there. I want to see his reaction when he sees her. I'll be as quick as I can with Hewitt, but keep him occupied until I arrive.'

'Fine, boss,' replied Watson.

If the truth was known PC Tyler would not have been Carmichael's choice to collect Bradley Monroe from the airport, however, he was all the duty sergeant could spare that morning. In Carmichael's view Tyler was not a bad officer. He always appeared to be keen. He would follow directives without question and he did have more than ten years' experience behind him. It was just that at times, in Carmichael's view, he came across as being a little arrogant and Steve had concerns about Tyler's lack of thoroughness. It would be going a little too far to say that Steve disliked Tyler, but his preference was to work with officers who demonstrated more care in their work than he had seen from PC Tyler in the previous dealings he had had with him.

As PC Tyler waited patiently at arrivals, he held up an A4 piece of paper with the name

Bradley Monroe written on it in black marker pen. A home-made sign that he had scribbled himself when he arrived at the airport that morning.

It took about twenty minutes for Monroe to clear customs, collect his bag and walk out into the arrivals hall. PC Tyler escorted his passenger through the arrivals hall and out into the drop off point where his police car was waiting. Monroe placed his bag on the back seat next to him and the car sped off towards the mortuary.

Carmichael arrived at the hospital after briefing Chief Inspector Hewitt about the investigation, and was astonished to see that Watson was still waiting for Bradley Monroe to arrive.

'I expected them to be here by now,' exclaimed Carmichael as he looked at his watch. 'Let's use the time we have to work out how we handle this morning.'

'Fine,' replied Watson, although he was not sure what there was to plan.

'When he arrives we should do the ID then, assuming we establish it is Lillia, we need to get a look inside their house. So we should try to take him back there and conduct a low-key interview,' announced Carmichael.

'Do you think he is a suspect?' asked Watson.

'Well, most murders are carried out within the family, so we can't rule him out,' Steve replied. 'It really depends on when he went to Frankfurt. If he went out before Saturday he has a pretty solid alibi.'

'He could have flown back, killed her and then flown out again,' Watson suggested.

'Yes, I suppose he could,' replied Steve. 'We'll need to check out his flights and also his itinerary when he was in Frankfurt. If he cannot account for any period of more than seven or eight hours, then we need to check flights to see if it would have been possible for him to make the return trip.'

It was a further twenty minutes before PC Tyler drove into the hospital car park.

Bradley Monroe was not what Carmichael had imagined. In truth Steve had not given much thought to what Lillia's husband would look like, but he knew two things about him. Firstly, he was a rugby player and secondly, he was married to a young and good-looking woman. So when a short, thin figure in his late thirties emerged down the corridor next to PC Tyler, Steve was very surprised.

'Mr Monroe,' Steve said as they reached

61

him and Watson, 'I'm Inspector Carmichael, we spoke on the phone last night.'

'Hello, Inspector,' replied Monroe without any real emotion.

'Would you care for a drink before we go in?' he asked, although he hoped that Monroe would say no.

'No thank you,' replied Monroe. 'If it's all the same to you, I'd just like to get this over with.'

Steve could understand this reaction and suspected that he would be saying the same thing, had their roles been reversed. Watson and PC Tyler waited outside as Carmichael ushered Bradley Monroe into the small viewing room. With the exception of the body lying still and cold covered up to its neck with a white sheet, the room was completely bare.

Bradley Monroe stood a few inches away from the bed. 'Yes, this is Lillia,' he quietly mumbled.

'Would you like to be alone with your wife for a moment?' Steve asked.

'Yes, please, if I could just have a few moments,' replied Monroe.

Bradley Monroe spent about fifteen minutes with his wife before he emerged back into the corridor. He looked pale and weak, but it did not look as though he had shed any tears whilst being alone with Lillia.

'I'm so sorry,' Watson said as Monroe moved towards him. 'Would you like us to drive you home now?'

Monroe at first did not answer, but eventually nodded and said, 'Yes, that would be very kind of you.'

Paul Cooper and Rachel Dalton had remained at the station after the morning briefing. Although the details of Lillia's missing car had been circulated to officers in the district, as yet there had been no reports of her red Audi TT being sighted in the area.

'The first thing we should do is check all the public and hotel car parks in a five-mile radius of the lake,' said Cooper.

Rachel unfolded a map of Harpers Lake and started looking closely at the area surrounding where the body was found. 'Well,' she said after studying it for a few seconds, 'it's pretty secluded, but there are a number of smallish parking places off the main road. We could start with them.'

Cooper peered over her shoulder. 'Yes, and there's a couple of hotels in the area which may have car parks.'

Rachel neatly folded back the map and the two officers made their way to Cooper's car.

'We could use my car if you'd like?' said Rachel, who never felt safe in Cooper's Rover.

'That's fine with me,' replied Cooper, who was oblivious to Rachel's evident aversion to his beaten-up, but much-loved friend.

It took the three men twenty minutes to get from the hospital to Monroe's house. Although both Carmichael and Watson tried their best to engage Bradley Monroe in conversation, for the majority of the journey they found it difficult to get much out of him, other than one-word answers. They were, however, able to establish that he had met Lillia four years before, when he was working in Tallin for his company. They also learned that Lillia was originally from a small town called Paldiski, which was about twenty miles outside Tallin and that she had no living relatives. Carmichael confirmed to Monroe that his wife had drowned, that it may well have been a tragic accident, but that at the moment they were treating her death as suspicious. What did surprise Carmichael was that Monroe did not appear to be shocked or concerned at these revelations.

Monroe's house was a new semi-detached property in a quiet cul-de-sac.

'Have you lived here long?' Watson asked as they walked towards the front door.

'We moved in here just before we were married,' replied Monroe. 'So about three years.'

Inside the house it was neat and tidy. Although it was sparsely furnished, the furnishings and fittings looked expensive and stylish.

'You have a lovely home, Mr Monroe,' Steve remarked.

'That was Lillia's doing,' replied Monroe with a smile. 'She had a good eye for detail and was very particular about how we should decorate and fit out the house.'

As Steve sat down he noticed a suitcase, which appeared to have been dumped in the corner of the room. Fixed around the handle was a Lufthansa label. 'Is that your bag?' Steve asked, pointing at the case.

'Yes,' replied Monroe. 'I just dumped it there when we got back this morning. I'll have to sort it out later.'

'So you came here on the way from the airport?' Steve said in surprise.

'Yes,' replied Monroe. 'Your colleague kindly allowed me to drop the case off here on our way.'

No wonder he was so late getting to the

hospital, thought Steve.

'Can I get you gentlemen a drink?' asked Monroe.

'That would be great,' replied Steve. 'I'd love a coffee.'

'Tea for me, please, sir,' interjected Watson.

Monroe disappeared through the door and headed for the kitchen.

'Did you know that Tyler had driven him here?' Steve whispered.

'No,' replied Watson. 'But we should have realised when he didn't put any bags in the car.'

'And we call ourselves detectives,' Carmichael mumbled. Marc just shrugged his shoulders.

'Look, when he gets back, you try to find out a bit more about their relationship and also his trip to Germany and I'll try and get upstairs and take a peek at their bedroom.'

'Okay,' replied Watson.

Lillia Monroe's shiny red convertible had remained in the isolated parking spot since she and her passenger had left it there on Saturday morning. It took Cooper and Dalton under two hours to find it.

'It's unbelievable that nobody reported

finding the car before now,' said Rachel. 'It must have been here since the weekend, and I can't believe that this car park has not had other visitors in that time.'

'Yes, it does seem strange,' agreed Cooper. 'But if nobody is looking for it, would they think it was worth reporting as being suspicious?'

'I suppose you're right,' concurred Rachel.

'We need to get the SOCOs down here to look for any evidence,' Cooper continued. 'Can you arrange that while I phone the boss?'

'Excuse me,' said Steve, as his mobile started to ring. 'I'll take this in the other room.' He picked up his half empty coffee mug and walked out of Monroe's living room to take the call.

'Excellent, Cooper,' he said as he sat down on the stairs. 'Once they have arrived at the scene, you and Dalton go and see if you can find where her body could have been put into the water.'

'Will do, sir,' replied Cooper.

Once the call was over Steve drained his coffee cup dry and crept quietly up the stairs, then silently pushed open the door to Lillia and Bradley Monroe's bedroom.

'When did you last see your wife, Mr Monroe?' Watson asked.

'Friday morning,' replied Monroe. 'My flight was just after eleven, so I took a taxi from the house at about eight-fifteen.'

'And was your wife her normal self?' asked Watson.

'Yes, she was on top form,' replied Monroe. 'She was very excited about an exhibition she was managing for Gemini in a few months' time.'

Watson could hear the stairs creaking and figured that Carmichael was making his way upstairs. 'Did she enjoy her work?' he asked in a raised voice, trying to mask the noise his boss was making.

'She loved it,' replied Monroe. 'She had done that sort of work before, in Estonia, so she was really chuffed when she got her promotion.'

'I understand one of the senior managers there is a mate of yours,' said Watson.

'Yes, Tom Sharwood,' responded Monroe. 'He plays at the same rugby club as me.'

'What position do you play?' Watson asked.

'Scrum half,' replied Monroe. 'I'm too small to play anywhere else.'

'One of my colleagues used to play,' continued Watson. 'But to be honest it's not a game I have followed. It was always a bit too rough for me.'

Monroe smiled. 'It's not actually as rough as it looks and the social is great.'

'Did your wife join in on the social side?' Watson asked.

'Sometimes,' replied Monroe. 'She used to come down a lot more a few years ago but not so much recently. To tell you the truth, she didn't get the game at all. They don't play it in Estonia.'

Watson leaned across to the coffee table and picked up his cup of tea, which was starting to get cold. He took a long gulp.

'Your boss is taking his time,' announced Monroe. 'What is he doing?'

Watson coughed and spat out a mouthful of tea onto his lap.

'Are you OK?' asked Monroe. 'Let me get you a cloth.' Monroe got up and walked in the direction of the hall. Before he could get to the door Steve emerged.

'Sorry about that,' he said. 'My colleagues have located your wife's car.'

'Where was it? Monroe asked.

'In a small car park by the lake,' he replied. 'They are at the scene now.'

Watson was still coughing. 'Are you OK,

Marc?' Carmichael asked.

'Some tea went down the wrong way,' replied Watson, who was still trying to clear his throat.

'I'm not sure what more I can do to help you,' said Monroe. 'But if there is anything just let me know.'

'There's just one thing more,' said Watson, who had just about sorted himself out. 'Can you supply us with a full itinerary of your trip to Frankfurt?'

Monroe looked at Carmichael in horror. 'Am I a suspect?' he asked in a raised and indignant voice.

'No, not at all,' replied Steve. 'But we do need to establish all the facts, that's all.'

This did not pacify Monroe at all. 'I cannot believe this. My wife is dead, probably murdered and you are only interested in my movements, even though I was four hundred miles away in another country.'

'Don't be alarmed, Mr Monroe,' Steve said, trying to be calm and reassuring. 'This is normal police procedure. There is absolutely nothing for you to worry about.'

Monroe appeared a little more comfortable on hearing this. 'OK,' he said. 'If it's all right with you I'll write it all down and either drop it into the station or, if you would prefer, email it to you.'

'An email would be fine,' replied Watson as he handed Monroe his card. 'Here is my work email, send it there.'

'Unless there is anything else, gentlemen,' Monroe said, 'I'd really like to have a little time to myself.'

'Of course,' replied Watson sympathetically. 'We'll leave you in peace.' Carmichael and Watson headed for the front door.

As they left Steve turned and shook Monroe by the hand. 'I'm really sorry for your loss,' he said with true sincerity. 'I promise you that we will leave no stone unturned until we get to the truth.'

Monroe was much calmer now. 'Thank you,' he said quietly as he closed the door.

Chapter 9

There was a buzz of excitement in the briefing room as the four officers gathered for their three o'clock meeting.

'OK, let me start,' said Carmichael in a loud, authoritative voice. 'Bradley Monroe has made a positive ID on the body. So we are now sure that it is Lillia Monroe. He maintains that he was out of the country since last Friday and, given that Stock has indicated that Lillia died on Saturday at the earliest, that means that if his story is correct, then Monroe is unlikely to have been involved.'

'He's already emailed over his itinerary for the trip,' interrupted Watson. 'His note is very detailed.'

'Are there any periods during the trip that were long enough for him to have flown back, killed his wife and then flown out again without being spotted?' Steve asked.

'I've not studied it that closely but it looks pretty full,' replied Watson.

'You both were excellent finding the car so soon,' said Carmichael, as he turned to face Cooper and Dalton. 'Have forensics found out anything from it yet?'

'Not yet, sir,' replied Cooper with a slight shrug of his shoulders. 'They checked it over at the scene and it's now down in their lab.'

'What else did you discover?' Steve asked.

Rachel looked at Cooper and they exchanged a smiled of satisfaction. 'Well,' replied Rachel. 'We are certain that we have found not only the place that Lillia's body was put into the water, but also the weapon that struck her on the back of the head.'

'Really?' exclaimed Watson. 'Tell us more.'

'About twenty yards from the car park is a weir. The locals call it Harpers Weir. It used to be connected to a small flour mill. The mill has long since gone but the weir is still there and has a really heavy flow down into the lake. When we looked around that area we found an old piece of piping, something that was probably discarded years ago when the workmen erected the current railings. Forensics have the pipe now, but it clearly had traces of blood and hair on it. We cannot be sure yet, but it does look as though the pipe could have been the weapon used by Lillia's attacker.'

'Great work,' exclaimed Carmichael. 'But we should not jump to conclusions until forensics have conducted their tests.'

'But there's more,' said Rachel, who was bursting to continue.

'We found Lillia's handbag,' said Cooper. 'It was fairly empty but still had her purse with her credit cards and a small amount of money.'

'So we can pretty much rule out robbery as a motive then,' concluded Carmichael.

'Definitely,' replied Rachel with conviction. 'Particularly as her handbag was a

Radley bag too.'

Her three male colleagues looked per-plexed.

'Radley handbags are extremely expen-sive,' she continued. 'They cost hundreds of pounds.'

'She really did have expensive tastes,' said Steve. 'Is that everything now?'

Rachel and Cooper nodded.

'Great work both of you,' he said. 'I'm sure these finds will help us.'

'So what do we do next?' Cooper asked.

Steve thought for a moment. 'Tomorrow, Paul, I want you to go and liaise with foren-sics to find out what they discover in the car and on the pipe. You can also get onto local radio and the local newspapers to try and find out if anyone who was down there over the weekend saw anything that could help us. You could start that this afternoon. Dis-tribute Lillia's picture. If someone killed her in daylight he must have been seen.'

'Do you want me to help him?' asked Rachel.

'No,' replied Carmichael. 'We have a lot to get through tomorrow. I want you to go through Bradley Monroe's alibi. Check out his email thoroughly. If there is any chance of him being able to come back here over the weekend then I want to know.'

'Right, sir,' replied Rachel.

'You will need to get on to his company to confirm that his itinerary is correct. You will also need to get on to the taxi company that took Monroe to the airport to confirm the time they dropped him off, also get on to the local police in Frankfurt and see if they can help you to check out the hotel that he stayed at, and if you can contact any people he says he met over there then that would be really useful.'

Rachel nodded, she felt excited that at last she was going to be doing some proper detective work.

'What about me?' enquired Watson anxiously.

'In the morning you and I will pay a visit to Gemini,' replied Carmichael. 'I think it's time we talked with Lillia's bosses.'

'Fine,' said Watson.

'Call Mrs Andrews and make appointments for nine am,' said Carmichael. 'Then, in the afternoon I want you to go through the autopsy report from Dr Stock on Lillia.'

'Will you want another briefing tomorrow, sir?' asked Cooper.

Steve paused once more. 'No,' he replied. 'I want you all to keep me up to speed on how you are doing, but our next debrief will not be until Friday morning. I think you all need some time to get on to the tasks you've been given. Also I will be quite busy myself this evening and tomorrow afternoon.'

'Why is that, sir?' Rachel asked.

'Well, Rachel,' he replied, 'it's because I need to go through this.' With that Carmichael pulled from his pocket a thick black diary.

'It's Lillia's diary,' he said. 'It was in her bedroom in one of her dressing-table drawers. I've just glanced at it so far, to read it all will take quite a few hours.'

Steve drove home feeling very pleased with himself. However, when he arrived home he found Penny in a foul mood. It had not been a good day for her at all. Her cooker was not working and although it was under the manufacturer's guarantee, they had informed her that it would be at least a week before they could come out to look at it. To add to her woes, her son had just told her that he was not going to return to school after the summer holiday, as he wanted to stay working at the supermarket, and her eldest daughter was continually fretting about her exam results.

It took Steve about ten seconds to realise that she was not happy. 'Why don't we eat out?' he said, hoping that this would reduce his wife's anxiety.

'That would be great,' she replied. 'But unless you are thinking of taking all of us, I'll still have to get something for them.' As she spoke she pointed at Robbie and Jemma, who were in the lounge playing a tennis game on Robbie's new Wii console.

'Also I still have to collect Natalie from the stables,' she said grumpily.

Steve assessed the situation. 'Why don't I collect Natalie and on the way home buy us all some fish and chips?'

'That would be great,' replied Penny.

'Then after chips we could maybe escape for an hour or so down to the Railway for a couple of drinks,' he continued.

'It's a deal,' said Penny with a smile.

Steve had been to the stables before, but he had never had much of a conversation with either of the De Veres. When he arrived Natalie was still putting her tack away, so Steve spent a few moments with Hannah and a man who was introduced to him as Stan Foster, the trainer of their greyhounds.

'So you are coming to the track tomorrow

I hear,' Stan said.

'Yes,' replied Steve. 'We're looking forward to it.'

'Should be some good races,' the trainer continued. 'Not easy to predict winners though, so take my tip and invest modestly,' he said as Natalie finally arrived.

'Ready, darling?' Steve said, giving her a squeeze.

As he was getting into the car Steve looked back towards Hannah and Stan. They did not see him as they were totally engrossed in their conversation. Steve could not help noticing how close Stan was standing next to Mrs De Vere, and how Hannah seemed to be enjoying his company.

'Chips for tea,' he said to Natalie as they sped back towards Moulton Bank.

Wednesday night was quiz night at the Railway Tavern. This was something that had slipped Steve's mind when he suggested a quiet drink. Under normal circumstances he would have avoided joining one of the teams at all costs. However on this particular evening he was ambushed by Robbie Robertson, who persuaded Penny and Steve to form a team with the new vicar, a local farmer called Wilf Swarbrick (who neither Penny nor Steve had ever met before) and Sam Crouch. To be strictly precise, Robbie press-ganged only the first four team mates into playing. Sam Crouch, on seeing Barney Green in the team, took no persuasion at all to join 'The Bears' as they called themselves.

'The first round is Pot Luck,' shouted Robbie Robertson, who was always question master at these events. 'Whose was the first birth in the Bible?' he asked.

'One for me, I think,' said Barney as he scribbled Cain on the answer paper.

After six rounds with ten questions in each round, The Bears were feeling smug. Given that they were literally thrown together, they felt very pleased with themselves to have finished third out of six teams.

'One last drink, everyone?' said Steve, who had already had four pints of lager.

'Not for me,' said Wilf. 'I've got to be up early to milk the cows.' With that he rose from the table and left.

'Let me help you,' said Barney. The two men left the ladies and walked over to the bar.

'Sam Crouch,' gasped Penny. 'You've been flirting with the vicar all evening.'

'Too right,' replied Sam. 'He's just bloody gorgeous.'

Even Steve had noticed a little chemistry between Barney and Sam, as did Katie, who kept her poise, but was boiling inside.

When Steve and Penny eventually made it home it was just ten minutes before midnight. Penny was no longer in a bad mood, in fact she was totally relaxed and happy. And although there would be no opportunity for Steve to read any of Lillia Monroe's diary that evening, he could console himself that he had made his wife cheer up and had uncovered a previously untapped talent for being able to answer some unusual and totally trivial questions.

Chapter 10

Thursday 16th August, the date that had been on everyone's mind in the Carmichael house for weeks. It was a day that they had all been half praying to arrive and be over with, but also half dreading. If Jemma did not get the grades she needed, the potential repercussions that this would have on their family harmony was something none of them dared to contemplate.

As Gemini's offices were little more than fifteen minutes' drive away from Steve's house, he had instructed Marc Watson to pick him up at 8:45 am. With Natalie needing to get to the stables and with Robbie not working that day, it meant that, for once, the whole Carmichael family were up and having breakfast at the same time, an unusual occurrence on a week day. Jemma's face was white and she was shaking with nerves.

'What if I don't get the grades?' a question she had asked time and time again over the last few weeks.

'You'll just have to go on the game!' announced Robbie with no emotion. 'Not that you'd make much money.'

'Be quiet, Robbie,' snapped Penny. 'We'll have none of that sort of talk in this house.'

'What game?' asked Natalie.

'Just ignore him,' continued Penny, her eyes shooting daggers in Robbie's direction.

Steve put his hands on his daughter's shoulders. 'You will be absolutely fine,' he said calmly. 'You are going to get the grades that you want, I'm sure.'

'Thanks Dad,' replied Jemma.

'And even if you don't it will not be the end of the world,' he continued.

'So you think I may not get them then?'

said Jemma with a look of horror on her face.

'No, I think you will,' Steve said firmly. 'But in the absolutely unbelievable event of you not, all I am saying is that it's not as devastating as you think it would be.'

Penny had been through this circular debate with Jemma many times and could see that Steve was faring no better than she had in trying to reduce their daughter's anxiety. 'But my whole entire life is dependent on these results,' said Jemma. 'If I fail, then I'll end up stacking shelves in the supermarket like Robbie.'

'Suits me fine,' said Robbie. 'No homework, no teachers on at you and you get money.'

The door bell rang.

'Thank God,' Steve thought. 'That will be Marc for me,' he said.

Steve kissed his wife and gave his eldest daughter a massive hug. 'Text me when you get the results,' he said to her. 'They'll be fine, you'll see.' Steve grabbed his mobile phone and suit jacket and left the rest of the family to continue the discussion about Jemma's A level results.

'Don't forget that we're going to the races tonight,' Penny shouted down the hall. 'We have to be there by six-thirty, so you need to be home by five-thirty at the latest.'

Steve heard his wife, but did not reply. 'Morning, Marc,' he said cheerily as he got into the car. 'Right. Let's see what Marsh and Sharwood can tell us about Lillia Monroe.'

Carmichael and Watson arrived at Gemini at spot on nine o'clock. They decided in the car to speak with Marsh and Sharwood separately, with Marsh being the first they would meet that morning.

The handsome, albeit slightly overweight, middle-aged business man rose from his chair, walked out from behind his large oak desk and stretched out his hand.

'Hello, please allow me to introduce myself,' he said, 'I'm Ralf Marsh.'

Steve took hold of Marsh's hand. 'Good morning, Mr Marsh,' he replied. 'I'm Inspector Carmichael and this is my colleague, Sergeant Watson.'

Steve quickly discovered that Marsh was a man who was used to being in control. Throughout their twenty-minute interview Marsh remained relaxed and assured. He was clearly upset by the death of Lillia Monroe, but did not give Carmichael or Watson the slightest indication that her passing would cause any major disruption to his business, or indeed to him from a personal perspective.

Initially Steve asked Marsh to give him a little background on Lillia and to describe her position at Gemini. Marsh pretty much confirmed what Mrs Andrews had said the day before, namely that Lillia had been at Gemini for about two years, and that she had been promoted from the sales office on the recommendation of Tom Sharwood. Although Marsh indicated that he had initially been uneasy about this promotion, Lillia had quickly proved herself and he felt that she did a good job in her new role, which he said was much more suited to her outgoing personality. Marsh explained that he did not socialise with Lillia out of work, but believed that she had settled well into life in the UK and understood that she was popular with her husband's friends and was often at social events at the local rugby club.

'To get more information about her out of work I suggest you ask Tom,' said Marsh. 'He and Lillia's husband are quite friendly, I think.'

'So when did you last see her?' Carmichael asked.

'It would be on Friday evening,' replied Marsh. 'Most of the people here left at two-thirty on Friday, but Lillia stayed on until about four or five o'clock, working on our most important annual UK exhibition. It's happening in October in Brighton.'

'Can you tell us a little bit more about what she did here?' Watson asked.

'She was our Communications Manager,' replied Marsh. 'In a small company like this it really means managing promotions, PR, exhibitions and the production of promotional literature.'

'Did anyone report to her, or did she have an assistant?' continued Watson.

'No,' replied Marsh. 'She got help from Ruth when needed, but she worked alone most of the time.'

As Steve had heard all this before from Mrs Andrews, he was keen to move the conversation on to other areas. 'Was it normal for her to stay late on a Friday?'

'Not really,' replied Marsh. 'She usually did get off promptly on Fridays, but I think that her husband had flown out of the country that morning, and she did not appear to be in any great rush to get home.'

'And what time did you leave, sir?' Watson asked.

'Much later, I'm afraid, much to my wife's annoyance,' replied Marsh with a frown. 'It would have been about seven o'clock.'

'And apart from you, was Lillia the last to leave?' continued Watson.

'Yes,' said Marsh. 'Tom is normally here late on Fridays, but last week he had to go to Manchester to extract some money from a customer of ours.'

'Can you think of any reason why anyone would want to harm Lillia?' Watson asked.

'None whatsoever,' replied Marsh without any hesitation. 'In fact she was very likeable, and I would have thought, with her looks, very popular, certainly with men.'

Steve smiled. Just about every man that he had talked to about Lillia, seemed to make reference to her looks.

'Do you suspect that she was murdered?' asked Marsh.

'We don't know,' Carmichael responded, trying hard not to give anything away. 'We are keeping an open mind on the cause of her death at the moment.'

'It's such a waste,' commented Marsh. 'How is her husband taking this?'

'He's very distraught, as you can imagine,' replied Steve.

'I will call him, of course,' said Marsh, 'to

see what help Gemini can be to him at this sad time.'

'I'm sure he'll appreciate that,' said Steve. 'Thank you for your time, Mr Marsh.'

'Not at all,' said Marsh. 'If there is anything else please don't hesitate to contact me.'

'Thanks,' replied Steve as he shook the hand of Marsh again. 'Actually there is one thing,' he remarked. 'With Lillia's death, who will be managing the Brighton Exhibition?'

Marsh looked surprised. 'Ruth Andrews will be more than able to cope. It was part of her role before Lillia was promoted, so she is more than capable of filling the void in that respect.'

Carmichael and Watson left Marsh's office and walked a few paces across the corridor to Tom Sharwood's office. Tom Sharwood was very different from Marsh. He looked about fifteen years younger and was clearly in good physical shape. He stood over six feet tall, had broad shoulders and looked as if he did not have an ounce of unwanted fat on him. However, despite his position and appearance, he lacked the presence and the polish of his MD, and was certainly more ruffled by Lillia's death than his boss had appeared.

'I just cannot believe she's dead,' he said. 'Bradley must be absolutely devastated.'

'Was theirs a strong relationship?' Steve asked.

'He worshipped her,' replied Sharwood without hesitation.

'And was this reciprocated?' Watson asked. 'Did she feel the same way towards him?'

Sharwood did not answer immediately. He seemed to need some time to choose his words. 'I think so,' he eventually replied. 'There was no doubt they were very much in love, but Lillia was certainly more independent than Bradley.'

'What do you mean?' probed Steve.

'It's hard to explain,' replied Sharwood. 'They loved each other and I am sure they were happy, however I never felt that Lillia needed Bradley as much as he appeared to need her.'

'I see,' responded Carmichael. 'But you would say they were happy?'

'Absolutely,' replied Sharwood. 'I'd say they were very happy.'

'When did you last see Lillia?' Carmichael asked

'On Thursday last week,' he replied. 'I was out of the office last Friday so it would have been Thursday. I did speak to her though on

Saturday morning.'

'Really,' replied Carmichael with interest. 'What time was that?'

'I think it would have been about nine-thirty or maybe ten,' continued Sharwood.

'What did you talk about?' Steve asked.

'There was a social on at the rugby club that evening, and she asked if she could come along with me,' he replied. 'Bradley was away and I think she was a bit bored, but didn't want to go on her own.'

'So what did you say?' Watson asked.

'I told her that I wasn't planning to go, but that if she was lonely she could join me for some dinner that evening,' continued Sharwood.

'Did she accept your offer?' asked Carmichael.

Sharwood paused again. 'Not exactly,' he replied. 'She said that she might join me, but that she was in a party mood and that she would try and see if some of her girl friends were up for going to the club first.'

'And that was the last you heard from her?' said Watson.

'Yes, it was,' Sharwood mumbled.

Carmichael thought for a few moments before continuing the conversation. 'Would you say that you and Lillia were close?' he asked.

'Not really,' responded Sharwood. 'We worked together and I liked her as a person, but I didn't really know her. She was just the wife of one of the lads at the club.'

Carmichael nodded. 'Did she get her job here through her relationship with you?' he asked.

'I'm not sure what you are implying,' replied Sharwood curtly.

'I'm implying that you may have helped a friend out by getting his wife a job here,' clarified Carmichael.

Sharwood started to appear uncomfortable. 'Well, in a way that is true,' he replied nervously. 'I did suggest that she may like to apply here, when I knew she was looking for a job. However I did not use any influence to get her appointed. Ralf Marsh does all the hiring and firing here.'

'So you didn't interview her?' said Watson.

'Absolutely not,' he replied. 'Not for the first job she had or for her promotion to Communications Manager.'

'But I suspect you did use your influence,' said Steve, as if this was a certainty.

'If you mean did I endorse her application to join Gemini and her application for promotion,' replied Sharwood in a raised voice, 'then the answer is yes. However, if you think Ralf Marsh would take someone on, or give them promotion, just on my say-so, you are wrong. Ralf started this business from scratch over twenty years ago and he still makes all the decisions.'

Carmichael again paused while he considered what his next question should be. 'Lillia was a very attractive woman,' he said. 'To your knowledge did she have any admirers?'

Sharwood thought for a moment before he replied. 'A few of the lads at the club fancied her, and certainly she was not shy in using her looks and charm to win over various people she came into contact with at work.'

'So she was a flirt?' Steve enquired.

'Yes,' replied Sharwood, 'that is exactly what she was.'

'To your knowledge, was she more than a flirt?' continued Carmichael.

'What do you mean?' Sharwood asked.

'Did she have, or could she have had a relationship outside her marriage?' said Carmichael, making sure Sharwood was clear about his line of questioning.

Sharwood became agitated. He could no longer look at Carmichael or Watson, and they could see that his face was starting to sweat a little.

'If I'm honest, I couldn't say for certain that she was not having an affair,' he replied. 'But I am not aware of her cheating on Bradley. She was a young, beautiful and outgoing woman. She did not appear to have any problems in using her looks to help her get her way, but I have no reason to believe that she was cheating on Bradley. As I told you before, Inspector, I worked with her and I play rugby with her husband, but I was not close to her.'

Carmichael decided to end this particular line of questioning. 'Did Lillia have any enemies?' he asked.

'Maybe some of the wives and girlfriends of these lads at the club that fancied her?' interjected Watson.

Sharwood shook his head. 'Not that I know of.'

'What about Mrs Andrews or some of the other members of staff here?' Steve prompted. 'She appeared to get promotion when, by all accounts, she was not the best saleswoman on the phones. Also, I understand that Mrs Andrews did the marketing communications here prior to Lillia getting the Communications Manager job. Was her nose not put out of joint?'

Sharwood could see that the officers had done some homework. 'It's true that a few eyebrows were raised here when Ralf promoted her,' he replied. 'It's also true that Ruth did not want to relinquish her duties in managing the exhibitions for us. Nevertheless, I do not think that anyone thought so badly of Lillia that they would kill her. Actually, if you must know, Ruth was very worried about her when she did not turn up on Monday morning. She even went round to her house that evening, she was so concerned.'

'I understand,' Steve said. 'We do have to look at all the possibilities though. I'm sure you can appreciate that.'

'Yes,' replied Sharwood. 'I realise you are only doing your job.'

'OK,' said Carmichael finally. 'We have no more questions, so thank you for your time.'

'Not at all,' replied Sharwood, who was clearly relieved that the questions were now over. 'If there is anything else that I can do to help, please let me know.'

'Actually, there is one other question you could answer for me,' he said.

'What's that?' replied Sharwood.

'Is it true that you were unhappy about the amount of money Mrs Monroe was spending on marketing for Gemini?' he asked.

Sharwood smiled. 'I'm the accountant here, Inspector,' he replied. 'It's my job to manage the finances and make sure we do not overspend. Lillia was not the most frugal person. She had no qualms about spending the company's money if she felt it was worthwhile.'

Carmichael nodded, smiled and shook Sharwood's hand. 'Thank you for your time, Mr Sharwood,' he said. 'You have been most helpful.'

Carmichael and Watson left the office and closed the door behind them. As soon as they had gone Sharwood slumped back into his chair, put his head in his hands and started to weep uncontrollably.

Ralf Marsh watched the two officers walk across the car park. He chuckled to himself as he observed the pathetic sight of Watson fumbling in various pockets for his car keys, before eventually locating them and holding them up as if he had accomplished some great feat. As the car containing the two officers disappeared into the distance, Marsh took out a bottle of Famous Grouse and a single glass from his filing cabinet and poured himself a large drink. He took a huge gulp of the golden liquid and slowly walked back to his desk and his comfortable leather chair.

'What did you make of them?' Steve asked his colleague as they drove out of the car park.

'I think Sharwood was lying,' Watson replied. 'He knows more than he was making out.'

'I agree,' replied Steve. 'I'm also not convinced that Marsh told us everything either. I don't know why, but I suspect that the answer to all this is something to do with Gemini.'

Steve's phone beeped noisily to indicate an incoming text message.

He scrolled through and slowly read the message. 'Thank God,' he said with genuine relief.

'What is it, sir?' asked Watson.

'It's Jemma,' replied Carmichael. 'She's got the A level grades that she needs.'

'That's fantastic,' Watson said.

'Oh, fantastic doesn't nearly describe what this means,' said Steve, the relief etched in every word.

Carmichael asked Watson to drop him off

back at his house. He didn't see any need to have another de-brief that afternoon, as he knew it would take Cooper and Dalton the whole day to carry out the various tasks he had set them at the previous day's briefing. He was also conscious that he could not be too late home that evening, as he and Penny were going greyhound racing with the De Veres and he desperately wanted to be there to congratulate Jemma on her results.

'You get back to the office and help Dalton and Cooper,' he said, as Watson brought the car to a halt outside Carmichael's house. 'Also, go through the autopsy report and make sure there is nothing in there that we have not yet picked up on.'

'Right you are, sir,' replied Watson.

'Tell Rachel and Cooper to call me if they discover anything important,' he said. 'That goes for you too.'

'OK, sir,' Watson said, and he drove off in the direction of the station.

It was shortly after 1 pm when Steve entered the house to find his wife and eldest daughter in jubilant moods.

'Isn't she brilliant?' exclaimed Penny, her face beaming. 'Two As and a B. Isn't that fantastic!'

'Yes, well done, darling,' he said as he gave Jemma a squeeze. 'We told you it would be fine, didn't we?'

'I know,' replied Jemma. 'I was just so worried that I wouldn't get the grades I need for Leeds.'

Steve smiled. 'So how did your friends do?' he asked.

'They pretty much all got what they wanted,' replied Jemma. 'One girl may have to go through clearing as she missed out by twenty points, but her mum says that they may take her anyway.'

'Twenty points?' enquired Steve. 'I don't understand.'

Penny had explained the points system to Steve several times before but, not for the first time, it was clear that her husband had not been listening. She took a deep breath and attempted to explain the process again. 'They award points now for the grades they get,' she explained. 'When they get offers from a university, they are told they have to attain a certain level of points to get a place.'

'I see,' replied Steve. 'So what was your offer at Leeds?'

'Three hundred and twenty points,' replied Jemma. 'And I got three hundred and forty.'

'So why don't lend your friend twenty?' he replied with a smile.

'You fool,' replied Penny. 'Anyway, what brings you home so early?'

'I just wanted to be here with the family to celebrate,' he replied. 'I've also got to do some lengthy reading, so I thought I'd do it here rather than at the station.'

'Just make sure you finish early, as we are going to the race track tonight, remember,' she said.

'I remember,' replied Steve. 'In fact, I am really looking forward to it. I feel lucky today.' He gave his daughter another hug. 'Well done, Jemma,' he said. 'I'm really proud of you. I only hope that your brother does as well when he gets his results next week.'

Steve then headed off in the direction of the kitchen to make himself a cheese sandwich and a large mug of coffee, before heading up to his study to spend the rest of the afternoon looking at Lillia's diary.

'I'm not sure that Robbie's that confident about his results, Mum,' Jemma said anxiously. 'Do you think Dad will go mad if he does badly?'

'I'm sure Dad would understand,' replied Penny, trying hard to make her lie as convincing as she could.

Chapter 11

White City Greyhound Stadium was an imposing building. It had been built in the mid 1930s, when the popularity of greyhound racing was at its height. In spite of its age and it needing some urgent TLC, it still retained an impressive façade. Set high on the wall some 20 feet high and 30 feet wide, was a brightly lit neon dog in full flight, surrounded with the stadium's name emblazoned in red, orange and yellow.

Steve and Penny drove into the owners' car park to be greeted by an attendant who ushered them to a vacant space.

'This looks nice,' Steve commented as he got out of the car. 'Where are we meeting them?'

'A restaurant called The Home Straight,' replied Penny. The car park attendant pointed them in the right direction, which took them through the double doors and up a steep staircase to the stadium's most prestigious restaurant. Once inside, Steve and Penny were greeted by Hannah and Charles, who were already seated at a large square table which had a commanding view over the finishing line.

'Wonderful to see you,' exclaimed Charles. 'Let me take your coat.'

Penny slipped off her coat and handed it to De Vere, who simply ushered over a waiter who took away the garment without saying a word.

'Please come and sit here by me Penny,' he continued. Penny did as she was ordered.

'We are really looking forward to this,' said Penny. 'We've never been greyhound racing before.'

'You'll love it, I'm sure,' replied Hannah. 'We've been coming for years and it's still so exciting.'

'Especially if you can pick a few winners,' interjected De Vere.

Steve was not a total stranger to gambling, but only in modest amounts, and up to that evening, only on horses. He was intrigued by the concept of dog racing but was not totally sure that this was really for him.

'How many races are there tonight?' he asked.

'Thirteen,' replied De Vere. 'They come thick and fast when it all starts, so you need to study the form in the programme well before the first race to stand any chance of making all your selections.'

De Vere handed Penny and Steve a programme each, which listed all the races and was packed with a whole host of information about the dogs' breeding and previous times and finishing positions.

'I may stick with nice sounding names,' said Penny.

'That's what I always do,' said Hannah. 'Although I do also pick out any that are Stan's dogs.'

'Stan?' enquired Penny.

'Stan Foster,' replied De Vere. 'He trains ours for us.'

'Are any of yours running tonight?' Penny asked.

'Yes,' said Hannah excitedly. 'Double Trouble is running in the tenth race. He's number six.'

Penny and Steve both flicked through their programmes to the tenth race on the card, which was due to start at 9:40. There they found details of Double Trouble, a dog that was only two years old and had finished first on three occasions in its last five races.

'It looks like a good dog, Charles,' said Steve, after reading its details.

'He is,' replied De Vere. 'But tonight he's

stepping up a grade so he'll have his work cut out to win. Hope he does though, as the prize money's not too bad and there's a handsome trophy for the winning owners.'

'So, would you recommend a bet on Double Trouble?' Steve asked.

'I suspect you'll get about four or even five to one from the bookies down there,' De Vere replied, pointing out towards trackside. 'So I'd recommend a modest investment.'

At that point the waitress arrived and handed out the menus. 'The soup today is tomato,' she said. 'Would you care for some drinks?'

'What will you have, Penny?' De Vere asked.

'A white wine spritzer, please,' replied Penny.

'And for you, my dear?' De Vere enquired of his wife.

'Well, I was rather hoping that we would have some champagne,' she replied.

'Absolutely, what a great idea,' boomed De Vere. 'Let's start with some bubbly.'

The waitress smiled and departed, returning a few moments later with a bottle of champagne and four tall glasses.

Over the next two hours Steve and Penny

enjoyed a wonderful meal in good company and could also celebrate a few winners on the tote. For each of the races, Steve selected his dogs based on studying their form and upon the times they had posted in previous races over the same distance. Penny's system was far less complicated. Her selection criterion was based upon choosing names that appealed to her. Much to Steve's annoyance, after the first nine races it was Penny's method that achieved the greatest success, having picked three winners to just one by Steve.

At precisely 9:33 the trumpets sounded and out marched the six canine gladiators for race ten. As with each previous race, they were paraded in single file in race order. In trap one, wearing the traditional red coat, was a large black dog called Twilight Time. The programme indicated that he was just back from a lay-off with an injury. 'He stands no chance,' commented De Vere. 'It takes a few races after a lay-off before most dogs are able to reach their potential. My boy will beat him.'

In trap two, wearing the blue coat, was a small white bitch with a black patch surrounding both its eyes. 'That's Director's Fantasy and she's fast,' announced De Vere.

'If she's out quickly and gets to the first bend in the lead, she'll be hard to beat.'

Then in trap three, wearing a white coat, was another bitch called Speedy Noir, who took the opportunity to relieve herself as her handler stood quietly by. 'I suppose that will make her more comfortable,' said Penny. 'But it's hardly ladylike.'

'I don't know much about her,' said De Vere. 'She's not run here before. She's come down from Middlesbrough, so I suspect her trainer has a high regard for her.'

Then came a very striking fawn-coloured dog called Rapid Ron. He was wearing the black coat and seemed the most relaxed dog in the race. 'He's no threat to my boy either,' remarked De Vere. 'He was good in his day, but he's nearly four now, so his best years are behind him.'

The fifth greyhound in the race was a small brindle-coloured bitch called Penny's Jewel, who looked raring to go in her orange coat. 'She looks beautiful,' said Penny. 'If she wasn't racing against your dog, Charles, I'd be betting on her.'

'And a wise bet that would be,' replied De Vere with a grin. 'She's the main threat to us this evening, that's for sure. I've seen her run before and she's very quick. Her problem is, though, that she runs very wide around the bends, so she loses time. But she's the one we have to beat.'

The final dog to be paraded was Double Trouble, an imposing jet black animal, who strode out with the air of an Olympic athlete.

'Isn't he magnificent!' proclaimed De Vere. 'If he's on form he'll have the beating of these.'

The stadium clock indicated three minutes to the off. 'Come on, Steve,' bellowed De Vere. 'Let's go outside and make a proper bet with the bookies.' With that he marched outside with Steve in hot pursuit.

Outside the warm and comfortable surroundings of the restaurant, the atmosphere was totally different. Here, in the cool evening air, was where the true punters lived. Men who, from their appearance, Steve initially thought would be relatively poor. It was only when Steve saw the amount of money that they were prepared to gamble on the race that he was forced to question this view.

When they reached the trackside Steve saw only five bookmakers. Initially they all stood with little activity. However, once the stadium clock indicated a minute to the start of the race, which corresponded with the handlers starting to load the dogs into their respective traps, there was a sudden stampede, with punters jostling to hand over their bets. In more than a few instances Steve saw punters passing over large bundles of twenty pound notes in single bets.

'Good God,' he exclaimed to De Vere, 'these guys must be betting hundreds on the race.'

De Vere turned to Steve and smiled. 'I'd say thousands in some cases.' With that De Vere himself lunged at one of the bookmakers and, to Steve's utter amazement, shouted 'five hundred pounds on trap six.'

The bookmaker took the bundle of twenty pound notes that De Vere had thrust in his direction and, after taking about two seconds to count it, stuffed it in his bag and handed De Vere a small betting slip in return.

'Not having a bet?' he shouted back at Steve, who was still completely shocked by what he was witnessing.

'Yes, I'll back number six too,' he replied. 'But maybe a more modest wager.' It was too late though, as no sooner had Steve spoken than the bell rang in the stadium to signify to the crowd that the mechanical hare was about to be started. On hearing the bell, the bookies, like synchronised teachers, wiped their boards clean of the chalk that had only a few moments before announced the odds on each dog.

De Vere strode quickly up a few stairs of the stand to get a better view of the race. Before Steve had a chance to join him the traps shot open and out leaped the six muzzled racers.

By the time Steve caught up with De Vere, dog number two had already arrived at the first bend, chased close behind by dog four and with De Vere's dog, Double Trouble and dog five close behind. As the greyhounds rounded the bends dog four and dog five caught up with the leader. By the time they passed the finishing post on the first circuit there was nothing in it between dogs two, four and five.

'One more lap to go,' shouted De Vere. 'Come on Trouble! Get up there!'

When they reached the next bend, dog five as De Vere had predicted, took a very wide path and as a result allowed dogs two and four to take a small lead. This lead was quickly caught up though when they hit the back straight for the last time. Steve could see that dog two was starting to tire and, as they reached the final bend, it was dog five who now led the race, followed by Double Trouble, who had also made tremendous strides along the back straight.

'Come on, my boy,' shouted a now very excited De Vere. 'Cut in! cut in!'

As the dogs hit the last bend, dog five again went wide, allowing Double Trouble at last to get into the lead. There was now only a matter of 80 yards to the finish and Double Trouble was clear by at least a length.

'He's going to do it,' shouted De Vere, who was now jumping up and down with glee. 'Come on, my son!'

It was at that point that dog three made her move. Up until the final bend she had never looked like challenging, but as they entered the final straight and as the other dogs looked as though they were starting to struggle to retain their speed, the Middlesbrough raider seemed to find an extra surge of energy. In a matter of seconds De Vere's face changed from a picture of delight to one of despair. Speedy Noir crossed the line in first place, with Double Trouble in second place and Penny's Jewel in third.

'That was so unlucky,' said Penny as the two men returned to the table. 'I was sure he was going to win.'

De Vere slowly sat down and said nothing. For the rest of the evening the mood remained subdued. Hannah and Penny tried their best to lift things, but in spite of their efforts and even though Hannah, Penny and Steve all had winners in the last three races, De Vere could not be shaken out of his all too evident misery.

When the last race finished and the bill appeared Steve whispered to De Vere, 'Please let me pay for the meal.'

To Steve's surprise De Vere did not tender any resistance to his offer. 'That's good of you,' was all he said, before making his way over to the cloakroom to collect the group's coats.

'We've had a really smashing evening,' remarked Penny, as she put on her jacket. 'Thank you so much for inviting us, Hannah.'

'We'll have to do it again,' replied Hannah with a clearly forced smile

'Yes, we will,' interjected De Vere.

After the customary embraces and handshakes, the two couples made their way slowly to the car park and away into the evening.

Five hundred pounds!' exclaimed Penny. 'He must be insane.'

'Yes, I suspect he is,' replied Steve. 'And

by the look of things it was five hundred pounds that he could not afford to lose.'

'Well, I won twenty-three pounds and twenty pence,' announced Penny with pride. 'How did you do?'

'I think I lost about fifteen pounds on the racing, and the meal cost me a hundred and sixty,' replied Steve. 'So, not as bad as Charles, but an expensive evening all the same.'

'Well, I think he's got a damn cheek,' said Penny angrily. 'To invite us to dinner and then allow us to pay just because his rotten dog didn't win. There's no way we're going with him again, that's for sure. And I'll be telling Hannah next time I see her.'

'Just forget it,' replied Steve calmly. 'No harm was done. There's no need for it to ruin your friendship with Hannah. After all, it's not her fault that he's a heavy gambler and a poor loser.'

'I suppose you're right,' said Penny. 'I'm just glad you're not like that.'

'With my history of picking winners I think you're safe in the knowledge that five pounds per race will remain my limit,' replied Steve.

It was a little after eleven o'clock when Steve

and Penny arrived home. At about the same time Bradley Monroe received an unexpected house call. 'What the hell are you doing here!' he exclaimed in a hushed voice. 'We agreed that you would never come here.'

His visitor remained expressionless. 'Are you going to leave me standing here on your doorstep?' he asked. 'I think it would be better if we discussed this inside, don't you?'

Bradley Monroe ushered his caller into the hallway. Then, having checked that there was nobody around to witness the visitor entering his house, he closed the door behind them.

Chapter 12

Steve could not get to sleep. In the semi-darkness of their bedroom, he lay open-eyed, listening to Penny's rhythmic breathing. The sound she made was neither loud nor heavy, but its recurring pattern made him irritable and, despite a few gentle nudges, his wife's metronomic noise continued unabated. After a sleepless hour he decided to get up.

'Bugger this,' he moaned quietly as he climbed out of bed.

Penny always slept on the side of the bed nearest the door. It had been her habit from when the children were small to leave the landing light on and the door slightly ajar, using a book as a doorstop. She did this so she could hear if any of them woke up in the night, and so they could find their way to her if they needed her. It was a practice that she still continued, even though none of her children had needed her at night for at least five years.

Steve slipped out of bed as quietly as he could, but the combination of him searching for his slippers and dressing gown, a few loose floorboards, and him banging his knee against the door, awoke Penny from her slumbers.

'What are you doing?' she asked in a daze.

'Go back to sleep,' he replied. 'I'm just going to get a drink and read up a bit more on the case.'

Penny groaned, turned over, wrapped herself in the duvet and slipped back into her deep sleep.

Steve had spent a long time earlier that day looking through Lillia's diary. It was a ten-year diary that she had started six Christmases earlier, before she had moved to England. Although on a number of days there were no entries from Lillia, when she did put pen to paper, she usually managed to write a fair amount. Unfortunately, but not surprisingly, most of the early entries were written in a language that Steve could not identify, but which he assumed was Estonian. It was only when she arrived in the UK that Lillia started to write some of her entries in English, even then these were few and far between, and the wording was usually very simple.

Steve had understandably concentrated his attention on the English entries and specifically Lillia's most recent inputs. The last short entry she had made was on the Thursday before she died. It was in English and read:

TF came into my office again. More nonsense about the money, but I will not change the way things are. I know what he really wants. I don't know why he cannot just let things be. Got home to find Brad in another mood. He says I am up to some mischief when he is away next week. He's such a child.

In her entries Lillia rarely mentioned people by their full name. She used various nicknames and initials. The most frequently

113

mentioned ones were TF, AS, PM, Lady Di, Lap Dog and Mutton. Steve did not know what TF stood for, but he assumed by the way she used it that TF was probably either Sharwood or Marsh, and she clearly despised him. She also consistently and mercilessley insulted the one she named Mutton. In fact the only ones who appeared to be people Lillia liked were Lady Di and AS. Lap Dog and PM only got a few mentions, and there did appear to be some fondness for them, but they too did have some unflattering entries at times. In one entry she wrote:

Lap Dog keeps asking me to dinner. I think he is serious about me. He is a sweet man but ugly. I think it is better for me to just do business with him.

And in another she had written:

I sometimes think that PM would have been a better choice than Brad, but he's not so good looking ... ha ha!!!

As Steve looked at the entries he saw a pattern in some of her movements. For instance, Lillia had AS against every Wednesday, which she had circled heavily in blue ink. On most

Fridays she had one hundred and fifty pounds written before any entry, and for the last six months on every second Thursday in the month, she had Lap Dog and five hundred pounds written next to his name. Steve also noticed that Lillia had not mentioned Lady Di for over two months, but could not see any reason why this should be. It was also noticeable that Lap Dog only started to get a mention about six months earlier, whereas the others went back for far longer. He decided that he would have to get a full translation of the diary before he could say for sure, as the entries in English gave him no clues.

Penny entered Steve's office. 'What are you doing?' she said sternly, but in a whisper. 'It's two in the morning.'

Steve put his arm around her. 'I'm reading through Lillia's diary,' he said. 'I think you may be right about her.'

'What? That she was a Russian call girl?' Penny said.

'Yes,' replied Steve. 'Well, a call girl. She seems to have many male friends, most of whom she despises, and there are entries here of amounts of money which make me wonder.'

Penny took the diary from Steve and read

through some of it. 'Good gracious, it looks like she earned at least sixteen hundred pounds last month if these figures are all payments,' she said in amazement. 'It makes my salary at the school seem puny.'

Steve laughed. 'Well, if you can work out who Lap Dog is and who was paying her one hundred and fifty every Friday, then they will be looking for a new...' Steve paused, trying to find the appropriate word to finish his sentence.

'Business partner is probably what you are struggling to say,' said Penny.

'Yes,' Steve responded. 'I suspect business partner most adequately covers what they were.'

'Anyway,' said Penny firmly. 'You told me you needed to be in the office early tomorrow, or should I say today, so I suggest we get back to bed.'

'On two conditions,' replied Steve.

'And what are they?' Penny asked expectantly.

'Firstly, I get half the duvet back,' he said. 'And secondly, you stop snoring.'

Penny looked at Steve in horror. 'I've told you before, I don't snore.'

Chapter 13

In spite of only managing to get four hours' sleep, Steve felt pretty good as he entered the station at 7:15 that Friday morning. What made him even more pleased was that he had managed the journey in a new record time, 28 minutes and 35 seconds.

'Morning,' he said chirpily to the desk Sergeant.

'Morning, sir,' replied the duty officer as Steve disappeared down the corridor.

By the time 8:30 arrived, Carmichael had been joined by Paul Cooper, Marc Watson and Rachel Dalton in the briefing room.

'How did you all get on yesterday?' he asked in anticipation.

Cooper was the first to reply. 'I have spoken to the local papers and we will be getting some coverage in their next issues,' he said. 'The *Advertiser* comes out today and they have promised us half the front page, including a colour photograph of Lillia.'

'What about the *West Lancs Herald?*' asked Watson.

'They want to come in today to have an interview with you, sir,' said Cooper, directing his gaze at his boss.

'What time?' Carmichael asked, although he had no appointments booked yet for the day.

'About ten-thirty,' said Cooper.

'What about the local radio and TV?' Steve enquired.

'We've had a good response there too,' he replied. 'The TV people are coming in to do an interview at eleven, and local radio want to do a live interview at about noon.'

'That will be tight for time,' said Steve. 'If I have to do an interview with the *Herald* at ten-thirty, I may not have finished by eleven.'

Rachel and Cooper looked nervously at each other.

'Well,' said Cooper carefully. 'Chief Inspetor Hewitt said he would like to do the TV interview.'

'Oh, did he?' said Steve. 'So he does the TV and I get the local papers and the local radio.'

Rachel and Cooper again exchanged an uncomfortable glance.

'To be precise, sir,' continued Cooper. 'The Chief actually said he'd do the TV *and* the radio interviews.' Carmichael's face turned to thunder.

'I think he felt that we should all be freed up to get on with the detective work,' Rachel said, trying to ease Steve's rage.

'But I also expect that Chief Inspector Hewitt will require me to brief him for the next few hours, so he doesn't look a tit in front of the camera.'

'Come to mention it,' said Rachel nervously. 'He did say that he'd like you to go up and see him straight after the debrief this morning.'

Steve shook his head. 'OK, OK,' he sighed. 'At least we will get lots of coverage, so well done, Paul. What about the forensic reports?' Steve asked.

'I've read all through the autopsy from Stock,' said Watson. 'There are no surprises. Death by drowning, blow to the back of the head prior to death, and most likely time between Saturday morning and Sunday morning.'

Steve was surprised that the report had yielded no more clues. 'Are you sure there was nothing else?' he asked.

'The only other thing Stock noted was that Lillia had no signs of any sexual assault, and that her body showed no signs of bruising. So it suggests there was no struggle,' replied Watson.

'So either she knew her killer or she was taken by surprise,' said Rachel.

'Or she just slipped and fell into the lake,' added Steve.

'Actually,' interrupted Cooper. 'That appears to be unlikely.'

'Why do you say that?' Steve asked.

'Because the forensic report at the scene indicated that the pipe we found was what caused her head injury,' replied Cooper. 'It also contains traces of fibres that were not from Lillia's clothes, but were also found on the passenger seat back rest in her car.'

Steve smiled. 'So, are we to assume that Lillia drove herself and her killer down to the car park? They got out, walked to the weir and then her passenger hit her with the pipe and threw her in the lake?'

'That is pretty much what the forensic boys think,' replied Cooper.

'And do they have a rough idea of the time this occurred?' Steve asked hopefully.

'It was certainly after nine-forty-five am on Saturday,' announced Cooper. 'Because we traced Lillia's mobile calls and that was the time of her last call.'

'The one that Sharwood told Marc and I

that he received?' Steve enquired.

'Yes,' replied Cooper. 'Lillia's phone records verify that she made a call to him at nine-thirty-nine am on Saturday morning, which lasted until nine-forty-five am.'

Steve thought for a while. 'Do the forensic people also give a time when the car was left, or for when the blood got on the pipe?' he asked.

'They say it has to be Saturday,' said Cooper. 'As the handbag we found had clearly been out in the rain, and it has not rained in that area since Saturday night.'

Carmichael grabbed a red marker and in big bold letters wrote the time of death on the white board.

09:45 am to midnight on
Saturday 11th August.

'That's a good start,' he said. 'Anything else?' Cooper and Watson shook their heads.

'What about the cross?' Steve asked. 'Has this turned up yet?'

'No,' replied Cooper. 'We didn't find it at the lakeside.'

'It's not in her personal effects either from the mortuary,' added Watson.

'She always wore it, apparently,' remarked

Carmichael. 'So I can only think that it was either taken by the murderer, or is lying at the bottom of the lake.'

'What about Bradley Monroe's alibi?' he asked Rachel.

'For Saturday it's rock solid,' she replied. 'He had breakfast at eight am in the hotel, with the hotel staff as witnesses, and he met with a new work colleague, Wolfgang Shultz from Frankfurt. Shultz took him for a sight-seeing tour of Frankfurt at ten am. According to Shultz this lasted until about six pm. So there is no way he could have come back on Saturday.'

Carmichael took his red marker and wrote on the board:

Bradley Monroe Alibi for
Saturday 11th

'How did you get on with the diary, sir?' Rachel asked.

'It's interesting,' said Carmichael. 'Most is in Estonian, but what is written in English paints a picture of someone who appears to be earning money, and good money at that, outside her job at Gemini.'

'Do you know how?' Watson asked with a grin. 'Or is that just stating the obvious?'

'No, Marc,' Carmichael said firmly. 'I really don't want to start jumping to any false conclusions, but at various times she has written some pretty significant amounts of cash.' Steve opened the diary to Thursday 12th July. Here she had five hundred pounds written at the top of the page and underneath the name Lap Dog.

'Lap Dog!' exclaimed Rachel. 'What does that mean?'

Steve shook his head. 'I'm not sure who it is but it looks like she got five hundred pounds from him on 12th July.'

Carmichael turned the pages to Thursday 14th June, where again five hundred pounds was written and the name Lap Dog. 'For the last six months on the second Thursday in the month she had written down five hundred pounds and Lap Dog,' Carmichael told his colleagues. 'And on most Fridays for the last twelve months she has written one hundred and fifty pounds down.'

Watson, Cooper and Dalton all waited to hear what else Carmichael had found in the diary.

'Also, on every Wednesday for well over a year, she has written AS, as if it's a regular appointment,' continued Carmichael. 'She very rarely writes about AS in English, but when she does it is usually done fondly, which is more than can be said for the four or five other nicknames and initials she writes about.'

Steve passed the book to his team who spent a few moments going over some of the entries. 'We need to get this fully translated as soon as we can,' continued Carmichael. 'That will be one of your jobs, Rachel.' Rachel nodded.

'See if you can get this underway this morning while I'm with Hewitt, and when I'm doing the press interview.'

'Ok,' said Rachel, as she snatched the diary from Watson's grip. 'I'll get on to it straight away.'

'Come back here at noon, as this afternoon you and I will go round to see Bradley Monroe again,' he said. 'Maybe he can shed some light on who the people were that Lillia was writing about.' Rachel Dalton left the briefing room.

Carmichael turned to Watson and Cooper: 'I want you both to go back to Gemini,' he said. 'Talk with Ruth Andrews, Tom Sharwood and Ralf Marsh. Find out more about Lillia's private life. They must know more than they have said. Also find out what they were doing last Saturday. And get Sharwood to tell you how much Lillia was earning.'

Watson grabbed his car keys from on top of his desk. 'I'll drive, Paul,' he said.

'If you're sure,' said Cooper.

'See you later, fellas,' Steve said as his officers made their way out of the briefing room.

'Don't forget to see Chief Inspector Hewitt,' Watson reminded his boss, with a smirk.

Carmichael heard him clearly but did not reply.

Penny's day started as usual by taking Natalie to the stables. She was still very annoyed that the De Vere's had allowed Steve to pay for the meal and was pleased not to see Hannah when her daughter got out of the car.

'Have a nice day, dear,' she shouted at Natalie.

'Bye, Mum,' replied her daughter as she ran towards Lucy's stable.

Penny watched her youngest child vanish behind the stable door before turning her car round and driving out through the large stone entrance.

Hannah De Vere watched as the car disappeared down the lane. She had been livid with Charles when she realised he had not picked up the bill and had planned to apologise to Penny that morning. However, the episode the previous evening had rapidly disappeared from her mind after she had picked up the *Advertiser* from her doormat, and had seen the face of her friend Lillia staring up at her.

Hannah stood shattered and frozen, her gaze fixed on Lillia's smiling face that beamed out of the picture. Tears ran freely down her cheeks and fell in mammoth droplets onto the local paper, which she had rested on the table in front of her.

'You poor young thing,' she said out loud. 'Who could have done such a dreadful thing to you?'

Steve took a deep breath and marched into Hewitt's office.

'I understand you wanted to see me, sir?' he said, as if the purpose of Hewitt's request was unknown to him.

'Steve, come in,' said Hewitt, who predictably enough was dressed in his newest uniform with a brand new gleaming white shirt, and shoes so shiny that it was actually possible for Steve to see himself in their reflection.

Carmichael spent the next hour going through the case with Hewitt in microscopic detail, which actually helped him to get his own thoughts together for his interview with the *Herald* at 10:30. As soon as Hewitt felt satisfied that he could command his media appearances with confidence his interest clearly started to wane.

'I'll not detain you any longer,' he said as soon as he felt able. 'Keep up the good work.'

'Thank you,' replied Steve, as he walked towards the door. 'I'll keep you informed of our progress.'

'One last thing,' Hewitt said, as Steve was just about to leave the office. 'As the media communications will start kicking in this afternoon and this evening, I think it only right for you and your team to make sure you will have full cover here over the week-end, in case we get callers about the case.'

Steve had already considered this, but had decided it was probably not necessary. His plan was to ask his team to leave their mobile phones on and he was going to instruct the duty officers to call him if there were any developments, but clearly this plan was not going to be enough for Hewitt.

'Absolutely sir,' he replied. 'I'll make sure that between Cooper, Watson, Dalton and myself we are fully covered on Saturday and Sunday.'

'Excellent,' said Hewitt as he brushed minute specks of dust from his cap.

Steve's interview with the *Herald* lasted no more than forty minutes and he was very impressed with how the young reporter interrogated him.

'What I am looking for,' Steve said at the end of the interview, 'is for your readers to contact us if they have any information that could help us. If they saw Lillia on Friday evening or Saturday, if they were at the lakeside car park on Saturday or Sunday and saw the car, or if they saw anyone down by the lake over last weekend who looked or acted suspiciously, then I want them to call one of my officers.'

Once he had finished the interview, Carmichael decided to grab a coffee from the station canteen, which was on his way back to his office. Unusually the canteen was fairly empty, so instead of taking his coffee back to his desk, Steve decided to take some time out to ponder his next move. As he sat there he noticed three uniformed officers arrive who were clearly in good spirits. At first Carmichael did not recognise them, but as they each made their way towards the tills he noticed that one of them was PC Tyler.

'Tyler,' he shouted across the room. 'Can I have a minute of your time?'

Tyler nodded and, having paid for his drink and bar of chocolate, walked over to where Carmichael was sitting.

'Sit down,' said Carmichael.

Tyler's colleagues left the canteen, leaving their friend alone with Carmichael.

'I just wanted to ask you about the pick up you made on Wednesday.'

'Fine,' replied Tyler.

'Did Bradley Monroe say much to you in the car?' Carmichael asked.

'No,' replied Tyler. 'He hardly said anything at all for the entire trip.'

Carmichael nodded. 'Was his flight on time?'

Tyler shook his head. 'No, it was about fifteen minutes late landing, but his bag must have been first off the carousel, as he came through arrivals really quickly.'

'I understand that you went by his house on the way to the path lab,' said Carmichael.

'Yes,' replied Tyler anxiously. 'It was almost on our way so when he asked if he could drop off his bag and freshen up I thought that would be OK. Did I do wrong?'

'No, not at all,' replied Carmichael. 'I was

just surprised that he would want to waste any time like that.'

'To be honest, sir,' said Tyler. 'We were only there a few minutes. We went into the lounge and he dropped off his bag. He then went to the toilet and then we left. We couldn't have been at the house for any more than ten minutes.'

'I see,' said Carmichael pensively. 'He didn't get changed or have a shower or anything like that?'

'Oh no,' replied Tyler. 'Apart from changing his shoes and leaving his bag he left pretty much as he had arrived.'

To Tyler's relief this clearly satisfied the Inspector. 'Will that be all, sir?' he asked.

'Yes,' Carmichael responded with a forced smile. 'That's fine.'

'What did you make of him?' Carmichael asked as Tyler turned and attempted to escape.

'Well, actually,' he remarked. 'I thought he was strange.'

'Why do you say that?' enquired Carmichael.

'Well,' replied Tyler. 'He just did not seem to be as distressed as I would have expected. It was as if he was just going through the motions. He did not say much but he didn't seem too grief-stricken.'

'That was probably just him being in shock,' replied Carmichael. 'In my experience, at first some people can appear unaffected by death, when it comes to a loved one, but later, when it all sinks in, they behave differently. I suspect now he is home on his own, he will probably really start to feel it.'

'I'm sure you are right, sir,' replied Tyler.

After he had finished his coffee Carmichael made his way back to his office. No sooner had he sat down than the phone on his desk rang.

'Steve Carmichael,' he said.

'Oh, hello,' said the caller nervously. 'My name is Sarah Pennington. I'm one of the receptionists at the Lindley Hotel. I have just been reading the article in the *Advertiser* about the lady in the lake. I'd like to talk to someone involved in the case if that's possible, as I know this lady. She comes here every week, but she's been calling herself Mrs Burton.'

Chapter 14

'Rachel,' Steve shouted across the office. 'There's been a slight change to our plan.'

'I'm going to have to go,' Rachel said to the person at the other end of the phone. 'I'll drop off the diary to you in the next hour.'

Rachel walked over to Carmichael's office. 'I've found someone at the local language college who is Estonian,' she said proudly. 'He said that if I get a copy of the diary to him today he will translate it for us over the weekend.'

'That's great,' replied Carmichael. 'We can drop it in to him on our way over to the Lindley Hotel.'

'The Lindley Hotel?' said Rachel with surprise.

'Yes,' announced Steve. 'I've just had a call from their receptionist. She is a hundred per cent convinced that Lillia has been staying with them every Wednesday evening for about a year, with a gentleman. They have been calling themselves Mr and Mrs Burton.'

Rachel opened the diary and studied all the entries on Wednesdays. 'That's when she has an appointment with AS,' she said.

'That's right,' replied Carmichael. 'Assuming Mr Burton is also AS, maybe we can find out from the hotel who AS really is.'

Rachel grabbed her bag and the envelope which contained the photocopied pages of Lillia's diary and followed Carmichael down the corridor.

When Watson and Cooper arrived at Gemini they were informed by the young receptionist that Ralf Marsh was out of the office and would not be back until Monday morning.

However Ruth Andrews and Tom Sharwood were both available. The officers decided to perform separate interviews. Cooper had not yet met Tom Sharwood, so he suggested he conducted that meeting, leaving Watson to question Ruth Andrews. Cooper conducted his discussions with Sharwood in the company boardroom, while Watson elected to use Lillia Monroe's office to question Mrs Andrews.

Carmichael and Dalton headed off in the direction of the local language college.

'Do you have any ideas on who the killer is?' Rachel asked.

Carmichael shook his head. 'My first thought in cases like this is always the partner. And I have to say that Bradley Monroe's manner and behaviour when he arrived at the morgue was not what you'd expect from someone who had just lost their wife. But his alibi is so watertight it can't be him.'

'Maybe it's AS?' Rachel suggested.

Carmichael nodded. 'Could be,' he said. 'But it could also be any of the other people she mentions in the diary. What we can be pretty sure of, though, is that it's someone who Lillia was happy to drive to the lakeside that morning and was also happy to walk with up to the weir.'

It was now Rachel's turn to nod in agreement.

Cooper and Watson left the Gemini building just before midday.

'So, what were your impressions of Sharwood?' Watson asked.

Cooper shrugged his shoulders and said, 'He told me very little really. He still maintains that the call he received from Lillia on Saturday morning was her asking him to take her to the rugby club that evening, but he also keeps saying that they were just work colleagues and did not socialise outside work. If that *was* the case, why would she call him?'

'What about her salary?' enquired Watson.

'She was on £23,500 per annum, plus the company car and free healthcare,' replied Cooper.

'Not bad for someone who could not have been more than twenty-five years old,' said Watson.

'She was twenty-seven,' Cooper said, 'but doing OK for herself that's for sure.'

'Did you ask about the names in the diary?' Watson asked.

'I didn't go into the diary,' replied Cooper. 'But he did make one interesting comment. He said that Lillia apparently did not get on with Ruth Andrews and that the feeling was mutual. According to Sharwood, Ruth thought Lillia was too young and inexperienced to do the communications role, and he reckons that for her part Lillia saw Ruth as a sad old woman who dressed like a person twenty years younger than herself.'

'Mutton dressed as lamb,' said Watson with a smile.

'Precisely,' said Cooper.

'So, do you think Ruth Andrews is Mutton?' enquired Watson.

'That's my guess,' replied Cooper.

'Well, it makes sense,' said Watson. 'And, as it happens Mrs Andrews has no alibi for Saturday.'

'Really?' said Cooper.

'She informed me that she is divorced and lives alone,' said Watson. 'Mrs Andrews maintains that on Saturday she was at home doing her washing and cleaning the house. She has no one who can vouch for her whereabouts until she went out to the cinema that evening with a friend. That was at about six-thirty pm.'

'I'm not sure she would be a prime suspect, though,' said Cooper.

'Why not?' asked Watson. 'She had effectively lost her job to Lillia.'

Cooper shrugged his shoulders again. 'It's possible, I suppose,' he said. 'But I don't really see Ruth Andrews as a killer.'

'Maybe not,' Watson reluctantly conceded. 'But she's certainly a possibility.'

'I think Sharwood is more likely to be the murderer,' Cooper said. 'He was with friends on Saturday, but from the time he took the call until about one pm, he also has no alibi.'

'But what would be his motive?' Watson asked.

'Don't know,' replied Cooper. 'Maybe he

fancied her and she rejected his advances.'

'So, in summary,' said Watson. 'Both could be our murderers, but neither looks that promising.'

'That's about the long and the short of it,' replied Cooper. As they drove back to the station, Cooper and Watson turned on the car radio to listen to Chief Inspector Hewitt's interview.

Carmichael was also listening to Hewitt as he sat alone in his car in the language college car park, waiting for Rachel to return after delivering the copy of the diary to the Estonian translator. Although he hated to admit it, Steve had to concede that Hewitt was doing a competent job.

'Is that Chief Inspector Hewitt?' asked Rachel, as she climbed back into the passenger seat.

'Yes,' replied Carmichael. 'But he's just about finished, I think.'

'My officers who are working on this case will be available over the weekend,' announced Hewitt. 'If anyone knows anything that may help their enquiries, no matter how small or trivial it may appear, please contact Inspector Carmichael or one of his team. They will be waiting for your call.'

Rachel fired a frustrated look at Carmichael. 'Does that mean we are all working over the weekend?' she asked.

'I'm afraid so,' Carmichael said as he turned off the radio. 'I'm coming in tomorrow with one of you and the other two will be working Sunday. I'll leave it to the three of you to decide who's doing which day.'

Rachel considered her options. She would have preferred to have the Saturday off, but the idea of a whole day of listening to Watson's sexist sarcasm or, even worse, the thought of a tedious day with Cooper, made it an easy choice.

'Can I do the Saturday shift with you, sir?' Rachel asked.

Steve enjoyed a smug feeling of satisfaction. Clearly this sensible young officer was keen to benefit from shadowing him. Something he could easily comprehend.

'Of course,' he replied as he started up the car.

Chapter 15

Sarah Pennington had a pretty face, but was the sort of woman Steve's mother would have described as being large boned. Her physique and deportment reminded Steve of the female drill instructor who had barked out orders at him many years ago at Hendon. However, in spite of her imposing stature, the receptionist at the Lindley Hotel was very softly spoken. And by the way she spoke it was clear that Sarah was well educated.

Steve suggested that they might like to sit somewhere private, and Sarah led them to some very expensive-looking sofas in the far corner of the foyer.

'So, you recognise Mrs Monroe?' Steve asked, once they had made themselves comfortable.

'Definitely,' replied Sarah. 'She and her man friend have been coming here every Wednesday for months.'

'And they registered under the name of Burton?' said Steve.

'Yes,' replied Sarah. 'We suspected that

they weren't married, well not to each other, but to be honest we weren't sure.'

'We?' asked Rachel.

Sarah blushed. 'The other receptionists and the waiters mainly, it's a bit of a game we play. We try to spot the couples who are having affairs.' Steve's expression clearly showed his surprise.

'We don't get that many,' Sarah remarked. 'Generally speaking, the Lindley does not attract that sort of clientele.'

'But you do get people who use the hotel for extra-marital activity,' Steve said, trying to be as tactful and as matter of fact as he could.

'Yes, a few,' Sarah said with a gentle nod of her head.

'So why are you so sure that the dead woman is your Mrs Burton?' Rachel asked.

'Because she was so striking in her appearance and also because of her beautiful cross,' replied Sarah. Carmichael at this point pulled out a photograph of Lillia wearing the cross.

'It's so unusual,' continued Sarah. 'Being candid, I was really envious of her having such a beautiful necklace and in all the months she came here I never saw her without it.'

'Tell me about Mr Burton,' Steve said.

'He was quite a bit older than her,' Sarah replied. 'I'd say he was about fifty, but he was quite well preserved for his age and always very well dressed. He wore expensive suits and always looked immaculate.' Although Steve was still a few years short of his fiftieth birthday, he did feel slightly taken aback that Sarah should use the term well preserved about someone not too much older than him.

'And how did they book?' Rachel asked.

'Always over the phone and always by Mr Burton,' replied Sarah. 'He would normally call over the weekend.'

'And how did he settle the bill?' asked Steve.

'Always in cash,' replied Sarah. 'That's one of the signs we look for when spotting assignations.'

Steve smiled. 'Would you be able to identify Mr Burton if you saw him again?' he asked.

'Absolutely,' Sarah said with conviction.

'What car did they drive?' Rachel asked.

'They always came separately,' replied Sarah. 'She would arrive first in her little red sporty car, collect the room key and go to the room. He would normally arrive ten or fifteen minutes later.'

'What sort of car did he drive?' Steve asked.

'He had a big businessman's car,' replied Sarah. 'Maybe a Mercedes or BMW, really big and expensive-looking.'

'Does the hotel have any security tapes?' Rachel asked.

'Yes,' replied Sarah. 'Mr Hamilton, the manager will be able to show you them.'

'Do you know when Mr and Mrs Burton were last here?' Steve asked.

'I suppose it must have been on Wednesday last week,' she replied rather vaguely.

'So that would have been eighth of August,' confirmed Rachel.

'Yes, I suppose so,' said Sarah.

'And would you still have the tapes that go back that far?' Steve asked.

'I'm not sure,' replied Sarah. 'We probably do. Do you want me to go and ask?'

'Yes please,' replied Steve. 'But before you do, can you tell me if Mr and Mrs Burton booked into the hotel for Wednesday of this week?'

'They did,' replied Sarah. 'But on Wednesday morning he called and cancelled.'

'What time would that have been?' asked Rachel.

'He spoke to me,' replied Sarah, who tried

hard to remember. 'I was only just on my shift so it would have been about eight am maybe eight-thirty.'

'Well, you've been really helpful,' said Steve. 'If we could take away the video tapes from the eighth of August that would be really useful.' Sarah Pennington got up and made her way over to the office.

'That's interesting,' said Steve. 'If Lillia was murdered on Saturday and it was by this Mr Burton I would not expect that he'd book the room and then cancel on the Wednesday morning.'

'I agree,' concurred Rachel. 'I think it's more likely that he only found out on late Tuesday or early Wednesday, and then cancelled the room.'

'That's what I think too,' said Steve.

As they waited for Sarah to return, Carmichael picked up a glossy brochure from the glass table top next to him. 'Look at the prices in here!' he said. 'The standard tariff for a double room for one night including breakfast is one hundred and sixty pounds.'

'If we are assuming that they also had dinner,' said Rachel, 'that would be a fair amount to pay for her company. And that's without any potential payments he made to her for her services.'

Carmichael pondered for a while. 'There were no values in her diary on Wednesdays, so I am not sure we should be assuming she was being paid for her company, not on her Wednesday assignations anyway.'

'Maybe, sir,' replied Rachel. 'But it's possible she did not record all her income in her diary, or maybe she received the payment in some other way.'

'Like what?' Carmichael asked.

'I don't know,' said Rachel. 'Maybe she received a gift or was paid by a bank transfer.'

Carmichael laughed. 'If Mr Burton is careful enough not to pay his hotel bill by anything other than cash, I am sure he would not set up a direct debit or do a bank transfer to pay for sexual services.'

Rachel, realising that her argument was weak, chose not to try and develop her theory any further.

'Anyway, how much do you think someone like Lillia would charge for a night in her company?' he asked.

Rachel shook her head. 'I have absolutely no idea,' she replied.

'It's got to be at least a couple of hundred pounds,' said Carmichael. 'And if so, it makes all this a very expensive hobby for our Mr Burton. I think that this was probably a genuine extra-marital affair. No money involved, just pure lust.'

At that moment Sarah walked slowly across the marble lobby floor. 'Here you are,' she said as she handed Rachel four VHS tapes. 'These are all the security tapes from six pm until midnight on the eighth of August. Two are just of the car park and two are from in here.'

'That's excellent,' remarked Carmichael. 'We will let you have them back once we've scrutinised them.'

'That's fine. Will that be everything, or is there anything else I can help you with?' asked Sarah.

'The only other thing we would like you to do,' replied Carmichael, 'is to come down to Kirkwood police station either later this afternoon or maybe over the weekend, to make a full statement and provide a description of Mr Burton.'

'I'm off on Sunday,' she responded. 'So I'll come down then if that's OK?'

'That would be fine,' replied Rachel with a wry smile. 'If you ask for either Sergeant Cooper or Sergeant Watson, they will be on duty and will be able to sort you out.'

The two officers walked out through the ornate hotel entrance and down the gravel path to Carmichael's car.

'I think I know what I'll be doing for the rest of the day,' remarked Rachel.

'What's that?' replied Carmichael.

'Watching some of these,' she answered as she held up the tapes.

'Maybe,' said Carmichael with a grin, 'but not before we pay another visit to Bradley Monroe. I'm still sure that he can help us much more than he has done so far and I want to ask him about the names in Lillia's diary.'

'Remember, sir,' said Rachel, 'he doesn't know you have the diary yet.'

'That's a very good point,' replied Carmichael. 'You can drive while I think of an equally good answer.'

Chapter 16

Penny hated shopping for food, but with her cooker still out of action, she decided she needed to stock up on microwaveable meals. So after dropping off Natalie at the stables, she made her way to Ainsworth's, the local supermarket on the outskirts of

Moulton Bank.

The first thing she saw when she entered Ainsworth's was the sight of her son loading cauliflowers and asparagus trays on to the shelves. Getting the job at Ainsworth's had certainly been a good thing for Robbie. It had enabled him to do something useful in the summer holidays and he was now earning quite good money for a sixteen-year-old. Penny was pretty sure that his shock announcement two days earlier, that he intended to leave school and work at Ainsworth's full-time, would not amount to anything, but she wished Steve would talk to him about it. She knew any discussions she might try would probably make him more determined not to do A levels.

'Hi, Robbie,' Penny said with a smile. 'How's your day been?'

'Fine,' replied Robbie curtly. 'What are you doing here?'

'I'm just getting a few ready meals to cook in the microwave,' she replied.

'I see,' he said as he picked up the two cauliflowers that had bounced onto the floor when he had slammed the crate down on the shelf.

'What would you like for your tea?' she asked.

'Don't know,' he said glibly.

Penny could see that Robbie was in no mood to chat, so she gave him a peck on the cheek and walked off towards the frozen food, leaving her son to wipe away at the spot where she had kissed him and stare back at her in embarrassment.

'Hello, Mrs Carmichael,' said a voice behind her.

Penny turned around to find Katie Robertson walking quickly towards her.

'Oh, hello, dear,' Penny replied. 'Are you doing the weekly shop?'

'No,' Katie responded, 'I'm just buying a bottle of champagne.'

'Champagne!' exclaimed Penny. 'What's the celebration?'

'I've been invited out for a meal,' she said with glee. 'By a nice fit man, and as he's cooking I thought I'd bring along the drink.'

'But you've got a pub full of drink,' Penny said in amazement. Katie pulled a face that showed there was a problem.

'Let me guess,' Penny said. 'Dad's not that keen on this man.'

'Not quite,' replied Katie. 'He doesn't actually know about my date. I'll tell him if it becomes more serious.'

'I see,' said Penny. 'Do I know him?'

'Yes,' replied Katie. 'But not that well.'

Penny waited to hear what Katie had to say next. When she said nothing Penny grabbed her by the arm. 'Come on, you have to tell me now,' she said.

Katie grinned from ear to ear. 'It's Barney,' she announced 'Barney Green.'

'The vicar!' exclaimed Penny.

'What do you think?' said Katie.

'I think he's very nice,' said Penny, trying to pick her words carefully.

Katie looked at her watch. 'Oh I'm really late,' she said. 'See you next time you're in the pub.'

Penny was astounded. She would never have thought that the vicar was Katie's type, and she could not help wondering what Sam Crouch would say when she found out.

When Penny arrived home the light on her answer machine was on. She pressed play to hear her friend Hannah's voice.

'Hello, Penny,' she said. 'Can you please call me when you have a moment? I need to talk with you.'

Penny pressed delete. She knew what Hannah was calling about and, although she attached no blame to Hannah herself, she was still angry about the way Charles had allowed Steve to pay for the meal the night before. She decided to leave making the return call until later in the day.

It was around 4 pm that Friday afternoon when Carmichael and Dalton arrived at Bradley Monroe's house.

'Have you thought about how you can explain away having Lillia's diary?' Rachel asked.

'I think I'll just ask if I can have a look in their bedroom,'

Steve replied. 'If he agrees I'll just find it and look surprised.'

'And if he insists on a search warrant?' Rachel asked.

'I'll have to think again,' replied Carmichael.

They need not have worried, as it was clear that Monroe was not at home. Despite knocking for several minutes there was no sign of the occupant.

'What now?' Rachel asked.

'Back to the station and a debrief with Watson and Cooper before we finally call it a day,' replied Carmichael.

Watson and Cooper had arrived back at Kirkwood police station several hours earlier.

They knew how Carmichael liked to work on big cases and had already started to compile the three lists that were now synonymous with a Carmichael case.

The first list was written in red and was what Carmichael referred to as his knowns. The second list in green was the unknowns, and the third was a set of hypotheses that Watson and Cooper felt were reasonable. This was written in blue. Each list was written on a large sheet of paper that they had torn out of the flip chart, and attached to the wall. On their known list they had eight statements:

1. Lillia Monroe was murdered between 9:45 am and midnight on Saturday 11th August.
2. Lillia was hit on the head with a pipe, then fell or was placed into the lake.
3. Bradley Monroe has a solid alibi for that day.
4. Tom Sharwood and Ruth Andrews have weak alibis for that day.
5. Lillia had expensive tastes.
6. Lillia had large sums of money noted down in her diary.
7. Lillia drove her murderer to the lay-by near the lake.

8. Lillia did not struggle with her killer.

On their unknown list they had just four questions:

1. Who murdered Lillia?
2. Why was Lillia murdered?
3. At what time did she die?
4. Who do the nicknames in Lillia's diary refer to?

On the hypothesis list they had written five statements:

1. Lillia knew her killer.
2. Lillia was an escort (hence the large sums of money she had written in her diary).
3. Lillia was murdered by one of her clients.
4. Lillia was murdered by either Sharwood or Andrews.
5. Ruth Andrews is Mutton.

Carmichael read the lists and nodded his approval.

'So, your visit to Gemini proved pretty useful,' he said. 'But what makes you think Andrews is Mutton?'

'It's just something Sharwood said,'

replied Cooper. 'He said that Lillia refered to Ruth Andrews as mutton dressed as lamb.'

'Really?' said Carmichael. 'That's interesting.'

'Is there anything else you can add to the lists?' asked Cooper.

'Under knowns,' said Carmichael. 'We can add that Lillia was in the habit of meeting a man every Wednesday at the Lindley Hotel. They registered under the names Mr and Mrs Burton.'

'Under hypotheses,' continued Rachel, 'Mr Burton is probably not the murderer.'

'Why do you say that?' asked Cooper.

'Because he booked their next Wednesday's assignation on the day we think Lillia was murdered, and did not cancel it until the Wednesday morning. Our belief is that he would not have acted that way had he been the murderer.'

'Makes sense,' replied Cooper.

Rachel picked up the marker pens and added these statements to the appropriate lists.

'So, what next?' Watson asked.

'Well,' replied Carmichael. 'Thanks to Inspector Hewitt we need to have cover over the weekend. Rachel and I are doing the

Saturday shift and you two are on duty on Sunday.'

'You're joking,' said Watson.

'Sorry, Marc,' Carmichael replied. 'But as a sign of my appreciation,' he continued. 'I am going to let you all go home early.'

'That's great,' remarked Cooper.

'But I want each of us to take one of these tapes that we got from the Lindley Hotel,' said Carmichael. 'Watch them this evening and call me if you recognise the man that Lillia was meeting.'

The three officers all took a tape and made their exits, before Steve picked up the last tape and made his way out of the station.

'Home early again,' exclaimed Penny when Steve walked into the kitchen.

'Yes,' he replied. 'But I'm afraid I've got to watch this tape at some stage this evening and I've got to work tomorrow.'

'Oh, surely not,' said Penny. 'I was hoping we could go out as a family tomorrow. Robbie's got the day off and the weather forecast said that it was going to be warm and dry all day.'

'Sorry,' replied Steve. 'I've got to be there. You can blame Inspector Hewitt.'

'So what's on the tape?' Penny asked.

'A full three hours of people coming and going at the Lindley Hotel reception,' said Steve.

'Sounds like a classic,' replied Penny.

'He looks so wooden,' Robbie said as the Carmichael family watched Hewitt on the local news.

'Yes,' agreed Natalie. 'You would have been much better, Dad.'

Penny didn't want to criticise Inspector Hewitt in front of the children, but she was in total agreement with them. When the interview finished, the channel was quickly switched to a music station by Natalie, who as usual had control of the remote. This was Penny and Steve's prompt to leave the room.

'I need to have a look at the tape at some stage this evening, so they can't hog the TV for too long,' Steve said as he and Penny sat in the kitchen.

'Let them watch their music channel for a while first,' remarked Penny.

Before Steve had an opportunity to say any more he received a call on his mobile.

'I'm watching the tape now,' said an excited Watson. 'You'll never guess who your Mr Burton is.'

Chapter 17

Shortly after his conversation with Marc Watson, Steve received a call from Paul Cooper. Cooper had also seen what appeared to be Ralf Marsh on his tape from the Lindley Hotel.

Steve was very excited about the breakthrough and did not want to wait until after the weekend to interview Marsh for a second time. So he was delighted to learn that the reliable Cooper had obtained the home addresses of both Marsh and Sharwood from Ruth Andrews at his first encounter with her earlier in the week.

'That's great work, Paul,' he said. 'I'll call Rachel later and arrange to collect her in the morning, and we'll pay Mr Marsh, or should I say Mr Burton, a surprise home visit.'

Penny overheard her husband's conversation and suddenly remembered the voice message that she had picked up earlier that day from Hannah De Vere. She walked through into the hallway and keyed in Hannah's number.

When Penny returned to the kitchen, Steve was already on the phone to Rachel Dalton. Penny signalled to him that she wanted to speak to him urgently.

'Hold on a moment,' Steve said to Rachel, as he put the palm of his hand over the receiver. 'What is it?' he asked.

'Hannah has asked if she can talk to you in the morning,' Penny said. 'She maintains that she and Lillia Monroe were good friends. She also says she may have some information that might help you identify her killer.'

Steve removed his hand from the receiver. 'There's been a change of plan,' he said. 'Why don't you come round to my house first thing in the morning. We will need to interview someone else before we call on Ralf Marsh.'

'What time do you want me to be there?' asked Rachel.

'Make it eight-thirty,' he replied, before ending the call.

Katie Robertson's date with Barney Green was going well. Unlike most of the admirers she dated, and there had been many, Barney seemed to have everything Katie was looking for in a partner. He was clever, he was charming and he made her feel very special.

He also demonstrated that he was no mean cook either.

'So why did you become a vicar?' she asked as she poured out the last dregs from the second bottle they had opened that evening.

Barney laughed as he took Katie's hand and helped her place the now empty wine bottle next to the empty champagne bottle on the table, 'I guess I joined the church for the same reason your father became a publican,' he replied. 'It's the family business.'

'Remember the pub is in both mine and my dad's names, so I'm a publican too,' Katie corrected him.

'That's exactly my point,' Barney slurred excitedly. 'And you are the next generation in the long line of Robertson publicans.'

'So is your father a vicar too?' Katie asked.

'Yes, he is vicar of the parish of Upper Wenvoe in Norfolk,' replied Barney. 'And not only that, but my grandfather was a Bishop, my uncle is a minister and so is my brother.'

'Blimey,' Katie giggled. 'So you must struggle to spend Christmas together as a family.'

Barney smiled, 'Yes Christmas is our busiest time.'

'Same with us,' remarked Katie. 'In December our takings must be at least double what they are in any other month.'

'It's the same with us,' he replied. 'Our congregations tend to increase by a fair amount on Christmas Eve and on Christmas morning.'

'I don't go to church much,' Katie slurred. 'Especially since my mum died.'

'Why is that?' Barney asked.

'Don't frankly know if I believe in God,' she replied honestly. 'And if there is a God, why did he give my mum cancer when she was only in her forties?'

'I can't answer that,' said Barney. 'That is the argument that I hear the most from people who struggle to believe as I do and I'm still trying to answer that question myself.'

Katie took hold of Barney's hand. 'But I will come and see your first service on Sunday if you want me to,' she said.

'I'd really like that,' he replied. 'I have to say though that I'm a bit nervous about it, but I expect the turn-out will be quite modest.'

Katie shook her head. 'You may be surprised in that respect,' she said. 'If there's one thing that you can count on in Moulton Bank it's that the people here are very nosy.

I suspect you may have a full house.'

'Really?' said Barney. 'I hope they know what they are letting themselves in for, as my way of holding a service is not what they may be used to.'

'I can't wait to see what you have in store for us,' replied Katie.

It was just before midnight when Barney Green said goodnight to Katie, outside the back door of the Railway Tavern. He kissed her gently on her cheek and turned to walk home.

'I'll see you in church on Sunday,' Katie whispered, before closing the door behind her.

Barney Green and Katie Robertson were not the only couple enjoying a romantic encounter that evening. Jemma Carmichael had fancied Mike Hornby for ages. So when he had started to show an interest in her that night in the pub, Jemma thought she had struck gold, and when at the end of the evening he offered to drive her the few miles home, she willingly accepted.

They agreed to park in a secluded lay-by on Tan House Row. As they cuddled up together in the back seat of his mum's Subaru Forrester, they were oblivious to the headlights of the car pulling up behind them. It was not until the police officers shone a torch through the window that they realised that they were being watched. Quickly the couple adjusted their clothing before Mike climbed out of the car.

'What's going on here?' asked PC Richardson, as if he did not know.

'Nothing, officer,' replied Mike nervously.

'Are you OK in there, young lady?' enquired PC Tyler as he peered into the back of the car.

'I'm fine,' replied Jemma who turned her face away from the bright light.

Having established that the couple were just innocent young lovers, the two officers told them to be on their way and waited by the side of the road as Mike Hornby clambered into the front of the car.

'Wasn't that the young lad who found the body in the lake the other day?' Tyler asked as the car pulled away.

'Yes,' replied Richardson. 'I'm not sure who his young lady friend was though.'

'Me neither,' said Tyler. 'Mind you, I must admit that I wasn't really looking at her face.'

'She was clearly embarrassed at being caught with her blouse undone,' continued

161

Richardson, 'but normally in these situations they try to cover up their modesty. She seemed more concerned about us not seeing her face.'

Tyler dismissed his colleague's comment with a laugh. 'Maybe she's just pig ugly,' he said.

Chapter 18

It was a clear, bright, beautiful morning. Rachel arrived at Carmichael's house at precisely 8:30 am, as she had been instructed. She gently closed her car door and walked slowly up the curved gravel path to Carmichael's handsome Tudor-style house. In the early morning sunlight the bright white walls, black wooden beams and cute little curtains that trimmed the windows depicted an image of pretty idyllic Englishness as well as any biscuit box or jumble sale jigsaw could portray.

'Good morning Mrs Carmichael,' said Rachel cheerily as Penny opened the door. 'You have a lovely house.'

'Thank you, my dear,' replied Penny with

a smile. 'Please come in.'

Rachel entered the hallway.

'Would you like a cup of tea?' Penny asked.

'No time for tea,' interrupted Steve as he came downstairs. 'We've got a lot to do this morning.' He gave Penny a passionless peck on the cheek and within seconds was out of the front door and heading towards his car.

'Leave yours here,' he shouted back to Rachel. 'We'll take mine.'

'Goodbye, Mrs Carmichael,' Rachel said with a smile.

'Goodbye, dear,' replied Penny.

Penny watched as the young detective dashed down the drive and got into the front passenger seat beside her husband. Although she had no reason to be suspicious of his relationship with Rachel, Penny could not get the thought of what had happened between Steve and Lucy Clark from her mind. Having been transferred from the Lancashire force to Durham a year earlier, Lucy was no longer a threat in Penny's eyes, but the shattering realisation that her husband had it within his make-up to be unfaithful, had now made her wary whenever she knew that Steve was working closely with a female colleague.

'So, who are we seeing before we meet Ralf Marsh?' enquired Rachel.

'We are going to see someone who says she knew Lillia Monroe very well,' replied Carmichel. 'She is also an old schoolfriend of my wife, so I know her too.'

'Who is she?' asked Rachel.

'Hannah De Vere,' replied Carmichael. 'She is the wife of Charles De Vere and they live at Hardthorpe Manor which is...' Before he could finish his sentence Rachel interrupted.

'I know the De Veres very well,' she remarked. 'Charles was a friend of my father's, but they fell out a few years ago.'

Steve had temporarily forgotten that Rachel Dalton was also a member of one of the area's wealthy landed families. 'Why did they fall out?' he asked.

'I'm not really sure,' said Rachel vaguely. 'I think it was a dispute about some money that De Vere owed my father, but I don't know all the details. All I can tell you is that they were very friendly up until then, and since then they have had no contact at all.'

'Really,' said Carmichael. 'So how do you think Hannah will react when she sees you?'

Rachel shrugged her shoulders. 'I really don't know, sir,' she said.

'It may be wise for you to remain in the car. If she has some information, I don't want her feeling awkward in sharing it with me due to some old argument between your respective families.'

Rachel nodded. 'That's fine with me,' she replied.

Hardthorpe Manor had been the De Vere family home since 1535. Although its sixteenth-century origins were still evident, the house and gardens had been significantly extended and changed from the mid-eighteenth century, thanks largely to a considerable injection of funds into the De Vere coffers, the rewards of the family's highly lucrative involvement in trade with North America and the Far East. However, the last three generations of De Veres had struggled to maintain the house and gardens in the splendor of bygone days. A combination of losses from poor business ventures and the heavy cost of death duties had left the De Vere family finances and Hardthorpe Manor in a sorry state.

Carmichael parked his car on the gravel drive and walked slowly up to the large front door. In years past he would have been greeted by one of a myriad of servants that the De Veres employed, however, those days were long gone, and the thud of the large brass knocker against the massive wooden door was answered not by a footman or housemaid, but by the lady of the house, Hannah De Vere.

'Good morning, Hannah,' said Carmichael. 'I understand that you may be able to help us with our enquiries into the death of Lillia Monroe.'

'Please come in,' replied Hannah.

Carmichael entered the massive hallway. Hannah closed the door behind him. She did not see Rachel Dalton sitting patiently in Carmichael's car.

'Let's go through into the sitting room,' she said. Carmichael followed Hannah across the tiled floor and into a large, well-furnished room.

Hannah was no oil painting, but she had a kind face and Steve had always found her to be pleasant and cheerful. She had immaculate manners and, had Penny not informed him that she was from common stock just like him, he would have guessed that Hannah was an English aristocrat who had been born into a life of privilege, and who had existed in an atmosphere of social advantage.

'Please sit down,' Hannah said. Carmichael sat down on a very low but comfortable sofa. Hannah De Vere then sat herself opposite him on a matching sofa.

'I just cannot believe she's been murdered,' Hannah said. Carmichael deduced that she had been crying. Her eyes were red and the skin underneath her eyes was swollen.

'How well did you know Lillia?' he asked.

'She was a really good friend,' replied Hannah. 'Well, so I thought.'

'So you fell out with her?' asked Carmichael.

'Yes, a few months ago, I found out that she and Charles were secretly meeting up,' continued Hannah. 'When I questioned her about it, she just laughed at me and told me that I was being stupid.'

'So you assumed that she was having an affair with your husband?'

'Yes,' replied Hannah. 'But now I'm not sure I was right.'

'How did you find out they were meeting up?' he asked.

'Charles has always had an eye for the ladies,' said Hannah with little emotion. 'He's had affairs before. So when I was told by some really good friends that they had seen them together in his car, on more than

167

one occasion, well, I just assumed that he was up to his old tricks again.'

'I see,' said Carmichael. 'And what did your husband say when you confronted him?'

'The same as he always says,' she remarked. 'That I was being paranoid. He completely denied her being with him at all.'

'And what did you do?' he asked.

'I told Lillia that I wanted nothing to do with her and that if I ever saw her with my husband again that I would...' Hannah stopped what she was saying.

'That you would what?' Carmichael asked

'I was angry,' replied Hannah. 'There's no way that I would have hurt her.'

Carmichael remained motionless. 'Were there any witnesses to your argument?' he asked.

Hannah dropped her gaze to the floor. 'I was in the bank at the time,' she replied. 'Someone may have overheard us. We didn't shout but I suspect it was possible that someone overheard what we said.'

'And that was the last time you saw her?' he asked.

'Yes,' said Hannah, who by now had started to cry once more.

Steve waited a few moments to allow Hannah to compose herself.

'But prior to your last meeting you were on good terms?' he continued.

'Yes,' replied Hannah tearfully. 'We were friends for about two years. Very good friends, I really liked her.'

'So do you have any idea why anyone would want to kill her?' asked Carmichael.

'Not really,' said Hannah. 'She was a lovely girl, attractive, lively, good company and was really popular.'

'Especially with men, I expect?' remarked Steve.

Hannah smiled and nodded. 'Yes, she had no shortage of admirers.'

Steve considered his next question for a moment, but decided not to hold back. 'We have reason to believe that Lillia might have been working as an escort,' he said looking to see what sort of reaction his question would receive. 'Do you know if that was true?'

'An escort!' replied Hannah in amazement. 'I don't believe that.'

'Wouldn't it explain her lifestyle though?' suggested Steve.

'I suppose it would,' replied Hannah. 'She did always have the most expensive clothes and was never short of money. I always wondered how she managed to do that, but

I can't believe that she was an escort. That's basically a prostitute isn't it? No I refuse to believe that Lillia was a prostitute.'

'We are not sure, but it's certainly one line we are investigating.' continued Carmichael.

'Well, if she was you'll find the details in her diary,' said Hannah, much to Steve's surprise.

'How do you know about her diary?' Steve asked.

'Because she spoke about it often,' said Hannah. 'She would tell me that all her secrets were in there and that when she was rich and famous she would get them published and earn a fortune.'

'Did you ever see this diary?' he asked.

'No,' replied Hannah. 'But she told me that even if I did I would not be able to recognise anyone as she gave them all nicknames. Well, that's except for mine.'

'She had a nickname for you?' he asked.

'Yes, I'm Lady Di,' she said with a faint smile. 'Quite a compliment really to be compared to the late princess, don't you think?'

'Yes,' Carmichael agreed. 'That's quite a compliment.'

Hannah took out a small white handkerchief and blew her nose.

'You indicated that Lillia was popular,'

said Carmichael. 'Was there anyone in particular that she mentioned to you?'

Hannah smiled. 'Yes there were two that she did talk about. Tom Sharwood from her work was one. She did have a bit of a fling with him a few years ago, and I think he helped her get her promotion. She lost interest in him though. To be honest I think she was just using him, she could be like that. Then there was another one. I'm not sure who he was, but this one she really liked, and I think it was her that was doing the running. She affectionately referred to him as her sugar daddy or Alan Sugar, so I took it that he was older than her and had plenty of money. I'm not sure his name was really Alan but I suspect he was married.'

Steve figured the second person must be Ralf Marsh, but decided not to offer up his name to Hannah.

'So was Tom Sharwood still keen on her?' he asked.

'So I understood,' replied Hannah. 'Lillia would often comment on how he pestered her to get back with him.'

'What about her husband? Did he not suspect?' Carmichael asked.

'I never really got to know Bradley. She didn't speak about him much, but when she did she was never too unpleasant, so I think there was still some sort of relationship there.'

'How did you get to meet Lillia?' Steve asked.

'When she first arrived in Moulton Bank she contacted me and used to help out in the stables,' said Hannah. 'In return she got to ride out on the horses. She would come here three or four times a week at first.'

'And was she a good rider?' Steve asked.

'Oh yes,' said Hannah. 'She clearly had a great deal of experience with horses and was an excellent rider.'

'So presumably, at that time, she was not that well off?' he asked.

'No, at first I don't think she was,' replied Hannah. 'She was always well turned out and tidy, but it was only after she had been working at Gemini for a few months that she started to be able to buy more expensive-looking clothes and start to live the expensive lifestyle.'

'I guess her lifestyle was enhanced even more when she was promoted at Gemini?' Steve asked.

'Well, yes,' said Hannah. 'She got that car, but to be honest she was living in style within a matter of weeks after she started at

Gemini. I suspect that she was just like many others you read about these days, funding expensive tastes on credit.'

Carmichael nodded. 'I suspect that was probably the case.'

'Well, inspector,' said Hannah, 'I'm not sure what else I can tell you, but if there is anything more I can do please let me know. Although we had fallen out, I did like Lillia and it is just so terrible to think that she could have been murdered like that.'

Steve stood up and gently shook Hannah's hand. 'Thank you,' he said. 'You have been very helpful.' As they walked back into the hallway the conversation turned to Natalie.

'She's a natural, inspector,' Hannah said. 'Horses can sense these things you know, and all ours seem to have taken to her.'

'Well, all I can say is that she seems to do nothing but eat, sleep and breathe horses at the moment,' he replied.

'I can think of worse things a young girl of her age could be doing,' replied Hannah, with a smile.

Steve nodded. 'Yes, I totally agree.'

Hannah De Vere stood silently in the hallway as she watched Carmichael's car drive through the large stone gateway. As soon as it has disappeared from sight, she walked down the corridor and into her husband's study. Charles was sitting at his desk reading the *Racing Post*.

'I think it's time we had an honest discussion about your relationship with Lillia,' she said. 'I suspect the good inspector will be back here again soon, so if you would like me to help you I think you need to start being a little more truthful with me.'

Charles slowly folded his paper and removed his spectacles. 'In that case, you had better sit down, my dear,' he said.

Chapter 19

'Did you find out much from Hannah De Vere?' Rachel asked as they drove away from Hardthorpe Manor.

'I'm not sure,' muttered Carmichael. 'It's clear Lillia and Hannah had been good friends, and it's also clear that her lifestyle took a change for the better when she joined Gemini, but I'm not sure we are any closer to discovering who the killer is yet, and I'm also not sure that Hannah was telling me everything. She knew about the diary though, and

I'm becoming convinced that the diary will hold the key to all this, so I hope your translator is burning the midnight oil on it this weekend.'

'He gave me his mobile number,' replied Rachel. 'I'll call him later to make sure he is.'

Carmichael had not taken to Ralf Marsh on their only previous meeting. Whether it was the cool way he had reacted to the death of Lillia or whether it was just his general manner, he was not sure. So based on the evidence on the tapes from the Lindley Hotel, Steve was now really looking forward to meeting the Managing Director of Gemini again, especially as this time it would be at his home and unannounced.

Marsh lived in a very expensive-looking converted stone barn perched on the crest of a small hill with a magnificent panorama of the West Lancashire Plain. On a clear day the view from his large bedroom window included not only the tall buildings of Liverpool to the south, but also the unmistakable landmark of Blackpool Tower to the north and the mountains of North Wales and the Lake District even further afield. As their car pulled up on the drive, Carmichael and

Dalton could see three young girls, all under the age of ten, playing noisily in the large garden that lay adjacent to the house.

'Let me do most of the talking, Rachel,' said Carmichael firmly. 'You just observe his body language, and let him see you taking copious notes. He lied to me last time and I intend to make him sweat.'

It was Mrs Marsh who answered the door.

'Good morning Mrs Marsh,' Steve said, holding up his identity card. 'My name is Inspector Carmichael and this is DC Dalton. Is Mr Marsh at home?' Although she looked shocked to discover two police officers at her front door, Mrs Marsh smiled politely and invited the officers into the hall.

'I'll fetch him for you,' she said before slowly climbing up the open staircase that led to the first floor landing. As she ascended Carmichael watched her closely. He guessed that Mrs Marsh was in her early thirties. She had a tidy figure and a pleasant smile.

'What on earth has Marsh got?' he whispered to Rachel. 'How does he manage to have two young, stunning women? He's got to be in his late forties or early fifties. What do they see in him?'

'Without meeting him I'm not sure,' Rachel replied. 'But money and power can be attractions, I'm told, to some women.'

'Really,' replied Steve as Mrs Marsh vanished from view.

'Not to me of course,' said Rachel with a smile. 'I just go for looks and a great bum.'

Steve chuckled. 'OK, point taken,' he said.

Within seconds Raif Marsh appeared at the top of the stairs, dressed in a pair of faded jeans and a loosely fitting jumper.

'Good morning, Inspector,' he said, trying to maintain his poise. 'What brings you here on a Saturday?' Carmichael could see that Marsh was nervous, particularly with his wife following just a few paces behind him.

'Yes, I'm sorry to trouble you at home like this, but there have been some interesting developments in the Lillia Monroe murder case, and the last time we met you did say that if I needed any further assistance from you I should not hesitate to contact you.'

'Of course,' replied Marsh, who by now had successfully negotiated his way down the staircase. 'When I said that, I did think that you would contact me at the office rather than at home.'

'I understand and I am really sorry to trouble you and your family on your day off, sir,' said Carmichael with a forced smile. 'However, I'm afraid that this cannot wait until Monday. It should only take a few moments of your time though.'

'Very well,' said Marsh curtly. 'Why don't you come through into my office?' With that he ushered the two officers into a small room.

'Maybe you could make us all some tea, dear?' he said to his wife.

'That would be excellent,' said Steve, who was keen to have their conversation without Mrs Marsh being present. 'I take mine with two sugars and just a small amount of milk, please.'

By the expression on her face, Mrs Marsh clearly knew that she was deliberately being excluded from the meeting, but she tried hard to disguise this.

'Can I get you some tea too?' she asked Rachel.

'Yes please, Mrs Marsh,' she replied. 'No sugar in mine.'

Once his wife was safely out of the way, Marsh shut the door of his office behind them and gestured to his guests to take a seat.

'How can I help you?' he asked as soon as they were seated.

'When we met last time you indicated that you did not know Lillia Monroe that well,' said Carmichael. 'In fact I recall you said that you were not in the habit of socialising with her.'

'That's correct,' replied Marsh.

'Then why is it that we have reason to believe that you and Lillia were in the habit of registering at the Lindley Hotel every Wednesday evening, under the names of Mr and Mrs Burton?' Steve said calmly.

Marsh placed his elbow on the desk in front of him and rested his forehead on the palm of his hand.

'Look, Inspector,' he said after a few moments. 'What I told you the other day was true. Lillia and I did not socialise. I admit we were seeing each other for one evening each week, but it was not a romantic affair and I was being honest when I told you that I knew very little about her.'

'Are you trying to tell us that during the many hours you spent with her, you never talked to her about her life outside work or her past?' enquired Rachel.

'Yes, that's right,' replied Marsh. 'I never asked and she never told me.'

'So how would you describe your relationship with Lillia?' asked the astonished inspector.

'It was just an arrangement,' he replied,

trying hard to choose his words carefully. 'There was no romance and no commitment on either side. It was passionate and at times intense, but it was not an affair.' Carmichael and Dalton looked at each other in amazement at what they were hearing.

'Let me get this straight,' said Carmichael. 'For some considerable time Lillia Monroe and you were meeting every Wednesday evening for sex, but you are saying that there was no romance and outside that one evening every week you did not fraternise, even though you worked closely together at Gemini.'

Marsh nodded. 'That's about it, Inspector. It was just a mutual desire.'

'And did this involve any form of financial transaction too?' Steve asked.

'I'm not sure I understand what you are saying,' said Marsh, with an air of incredulity.

'Then let me put it another way,' Steve said bluntly. 'Were you paying Lillia Monroe for sex?'

Both Marsh and Rachel were shocked at the directness of the question, as was Mrs Marsh, who had decided to loiter outside the door before entering with her tray of drinks and biscuits.

'Absolutely not,' snapped the indignant Marsh. 'Do I look like someone who has to pay for sex? I can assure you, Inspector, that I have never paid for sex in my life and my understanding with Lillia was based on a shared need. We both knew what we were doing and both enjoyed the arrangement. There were no strings attached by either of us and there were certainly no payments made.'

It was at this moment that Allison Marsh entered the room with her tray. She quietly walked over to her husband's desk and laid the tray down in front of him.

'Yours was with two sugars,' she confirmed with Carmichael.

'Yes, thank you,' replied Steve, as he took the mug from her hand.

'And yours is without,' she said to Rachel.

'That's correct,' she replied with a smile.

Allison Marsh passed over the mug of tea to Rachel and then took the plate of biscuits off the tray and placed it in front of her husband. Then without another word she took hold of the tray and turned as if to walk away.

Carmichael could not help feeling sorry for Allison Marsh and wondered what she would have said or how she would have reacted had she known what her husband had just been saying. He did not have to wonder too long. In one swift movement, with lightning speed and pin-point accuracy, Allison Marsh swung her right arm, still clutching the wooden tray, in the direction of her husband.

Ralf Marsh never saw the tray, until it had successfully collided with the side of his head.

'You bastard,' she yelled at him. 'How could you!'

Fortunately for Ralf, Steve had anticipated the second blow and managed to dash over and grab Allison's arm, before she had a chance to translate her anger into action once more.

As her husband tried to stem the flow of blood from his nose and from a huge cut that the tray had made on his cheek, Allison composed herself. 'I'm so sorry, inspector,' she said calmly. 'I'm not sure what you must think of me.'

Steve and Rachel said nothing. Both officers were still in shock at the speed and ferocity of her assault on her husband.

'As for you,' she said, looking straight at her husband, 'once these officers have finished with you, I want you out of this house.' Without waiting for a reply, she then walked calmly to the door and left the room, quietly closing the door behind her.

Although Marsh's injuries were not too serious, they were bad enough to require a visit to the A & E department at Kirkwood Hospital. Rachel was given the job of accompanying Marsh in the ambulance and sitting with him in the A & E waiting room for the three hours that elapsed before he was treated and released. Following his treatment, Marsh was taken to Kirkwood police station where he gave a full statement outlining his relationship with Lillia Monroe and his whereabouts on the evening of Friday the tenth of August and the morning of Saturday the eleventh of August.

In his statement Ralf Marsh maintained that he and Lillia had been the last people to leave Gemini on the tenth of August. Marsh claimed that Lillia had asked him to join her that evening at the Lindley, but he declined her request on the grounds that he would not be able to make a good enough excuse for his wife to believe, given the short notice. According to Marsh's statement, Lillia had taken this rebuff in good heart but had teased him that she would find some similar action elsewhere. Marsh maintained that he last saw Lillia at about 6:30 pm on Friday the tenth, when she left the office, and that, with the exception of an hour at the office in the morning, he had spent the whole of Saturday the eleventh of August with his wife and children at home.

After the ambulance had taken away Ralf Marsh and Rachel Dalton, Steve decided that he would stay to ask Allison Marsh a few questions. He found her in the kitchen, sitting on a stool and gently crying. She was still clearly distressed and angry, but as he looked upon her Steve found it almost inconceivable that the vulnerable, slightly built and attractive woman who sat before him was the same person who had so viciously attacked her husband less than thirty minutes earlier.

'Has he gone?' she asked.

'Yes,' said Carmichael calmly. 'DC Dalton has gone with him to the hospital.'

'Is he badly hurt?' she asked.

'I don't think so,' replied Carmichael. 'But I suspect he will need some stitches and may have a bit of a headache for a while. And I feel I need to warn you that, should your husband decide to press charges, you could face prosecution for assault.'

'I don't know why I am so angry,' she said.

'It's not as if this is really much of a surprise.'

'What do you mean?' asked Steve. 'Did you suspect he was seeing someone else?'

'Actually, no,' replied Allison. 'However, it's how our relationship started. I'm not his first wife, you see. I was once his children's nanny. Anyway, one thing led to another and nanny became mistress, then mistress became home-breaker and the reason for his divorce. And finally wife number two.'

'I see,' said Steve trying hard to sound sympathetic.

'So it should not surprise me when wife number two gets treated the same way as wife number one,' said Allison. 'I would imagine Helen, that was his first wife, would find this all very amusing and poetic justice.'

Carmichael did not remain too long with Allison Marsh. However before he left she corroborated the account that her husband would later give Rachel of his movements on the evening of the tenth and on the morning of the eleventh of August. By the time Carmichael left the house, Allison Marsh had regained her composure and had re-found her attractive smile.

'He may be a vain control freak, who is obsessed with his own power and an utter

185

bastard,' she said before she closed the door behind her, 'but he's pretty harmless. He's not your killer, Inspector Carmichael. I am quite sure of that.'

Steve said nothing. He tended to agree with her assessment of her husband, but was still not sure. As he returned to his car, Steve could not stop himself from again wondering what it was that made Ralf Marsh capable of being attractive to two young, intelligent and beautiful women. 'It must be his money,' he whispered to himself.

It was just after 4 pm when Ralf Marsh finally left Kirkwood police station. Although Carmichael had arrived at the station long before Rachel and her wounded companion made their entrance, he had decided to leave Rachel to take Ralf Marsh's statement on her own. He was sure that she would be able to manage this and doubted that Marsh would tell them much more than he had already. He also wanted to take the time to leave Watson and Cooper a note outlining their progress that day, and to indicate to them both what he wanted them to do on Sunday.

Steve allowed himself a smug smile as he watched Ralf Marsh walk slowly through the gate and towards the bus station. The forlorn figure, complete with a large white plaster on his right cheek, bore little resemblance to the self-assured person he had met a few days earlier at Gemini Technologies, or the man who had ushered them into his office that morning.

Steve did not hear Rachel enter his office and was startled when she spoke. 'Do you think he's our murderer?' she asked.

'No,' replied Carmichael. 'I don't like him, but I don't think he's our murderer.'

'Me neither,' agreed Rachel. 'Pity really, I'd like to lock him up.'

Steve turned back to face his colleague. 'On what grounds?' he asked.

Rachel shrugged her shoulders. 'I don't know. How about on the grounds of being a complete and utter pig?'

Steve smiled. 'Sounds fair to me, but alas I suspect the local magistrate's court may not share our views.'

Rachel nodded. 'She'll take him back though, won't she?'

'Do you think so?' Carmichael asked with some surprise.

'Oh, I'm pretty sure of that,' Rachel announced angrily.

'Why?' asked Carmichael.

'Because men like that are for some crazy reason a really strong magnet to some women,' she replied. 'Don't ask me to explain. I suspect it's the power they convey.'

'Well, he certainly would appear to have been just that to Lillia, so maybe he is to his wife too,' said Carmichael. 'However I'm not so sure Mrs Marsh will be as forgiving as you think. She is clearly very hurt by what she learnt today.'

'I hope you are right,' she replied. 'That man deserves to suffer.' Steve was taken aback by her final remark. He had not seen Rachel in such an aggressive mood before.

'Oh, I meant to tell you,' said Rachel. 'I called the translator earlier and he says that he has been through almost half of the diary. He assured me that he would have it finished for us to read on Monday.'

'That's great,' replied Carmichael. 'I'm certain that the diary will hold all the answers to this case.'

It was a little after 5 pm when Carmichael and Rachel Dalton arrived back outside his house in Moulton Bank.

'Would you like to come in for a drink before you go?' Steve asked.

'No, thank you, sir,' she said. 'I'm going

188

out this evening so I'm in a bit of a rush.'

'Well, have a nice evening, Rachel,' he said as they clambered out of his car. 'You did well today. I'll see you on Monday.'

'Thank you, sir,' she replied. 'I'll see you on Monday.'

Rachel decided it was probably wise to keep quiet about her date that evening with the good-looking translator, who had invited her out for a drink when she had called him earlier in the day. She was sure that Carmichael would disapprove of her mixing business with pleasure.

Chapter 20

The female members of the Carmichael house needed no chivvying from Steve on that particular Sunday. Not even the strong wind and persistent wet drizzle that greeted them that morning could dampen Penny, Jemma and Natalie's excitement about seeing Reverend Green in action. They left home earlier than normal, but the roads leading up to the village church were so busy that they arrived with little time to spare before the service was due to start.

'Where have all these cars come from?' exclaimed Steve, when he failed to find any vacant spaces in the car park. 'The whole village must be here!' Although his observation was slightly exaggerated, he was not too far adrift, and the congregation that Sunday morning included a whole group of people who would never normally make an appearance at church. When they finally entered the church the Carmichael family only just managed to find a vacant pew where they could all sit together. Those that arrived after them were not so fortunate and by the time the service began, there must have been at least thirty people who had to either stand at the back of the church, or locate themselves down the small aisles on both sides of the nave.

Among these newcomers were Sam Crouch and Katie Robertson, who, like most of the others, had come especially to see the first service of the new vicar of Moulton Bank. Penny nudged Steve when she saw them both.

'This will all end in tears,' she said.

'What will?' enquired Steve, who was oblivious to the fact that these two were both smitten by the same man.

'Sam and Katie,' Penny responded. 'They are both mooning over Barney Green. He seems to be showing an interest in both of them and well, it all looks like it's heading for trouble.'

'I think you're mistaken,' replied Steve. 'I suspect that he's not interested in both of them. He's probably just being friendly.'

Penny did not respond. At times she found it almost impossible to comprehend how such an unobservant person as her husband could have forged for himself a successful career as a detective. He seemed incapable of seeing what, in her eyes, was the blatantly obvious.

Having already met Barney Green, Penny and Steve were fully expecting his service to be unlike those they had attended before. However, the way he conducted the service was so marked from anything they had experienced before, that it surprised even them. Gone were the serious sermons that they were familiar with, gone were the traditional hymns that they were used to singing and gone were the robes that previous vicars had worn on these occasions. These were replaced by an unshaven vicar in casual trousers and training shoes, who played his guitar and preferred modern hymns. Throughout the hour-long service, when he spoke to the congregation it was unscripted, which was also quite unusual, and when he made references to support his words, he would use quotes from philosophers, songwriters and playwrights as much as from the scriptures. At the end of the service Barney thanked them all for coming and, to everyone's astonishment, invited the entire congregation to join him for a drink in the Railway Tavern.

'Sounds a good idea to me,' Steve said to Penny. 'Are you up for a quick one?'

Not wanting to miss a possible encounter between the vicar's two female suitors, Penny happily agreed.

When Carl Tanner carried out his first burglary, he was terrified. His heart raced and he could feel himself sweating throughout the whole time he was inside the house. However, as he progressed with houses two, three, four and five the whole experience became less stressful for him, and he actually started to get a kick from the adrenalin rush that his Sunday lunchtime activity was providing.

He was careful to always select houses where the back gardens were enclosed and where the back door was hidden from eagle-eyed neighbours. He only chose homes that had glass back doors or doors with windows, and he always wore gloves. He could not believe how easy it was to find his targets, and he was even more surprised at how quick and simple it was to break in, particularly those houses that had just single-paned glass in the back door windows. Using his normal method he had decided upon Bradley Monroe's house as his latest mark, a selection that he would soon come to regret.

The Railway Tavern was normally fairly full on Sunday lunchtimes, but following the vicar's open invitation, Robbie and Katie Robertson were almost overwhelmed by the number of additional people that had decided to join him.

'He could have told us beforehand,' shouted Robbie to Steve as he pulled his pint. 'If I'd have known I could have got more staff in.'

'Don't knock it, Dad,' whispered Katie. 'I bet we will have record takings today, thanks to Barney.'

At that moment in walked the vicar. As he made his way to the bar various people in the pub said hello, but to their surprise the vicar did not appear to be his normal ebullient self.

Penny stood by her husband and waited to see what would transpire now that Katie Robertson and Sam Crouch were both in the pub. Penny did not know how much each of his admirers was aware of the other's interest in the new vicar, but she was sure that this would become apparent to at least one of them within the next few hours.

It was Sam Crouch who made the first move. As the vicar pushed by her she gently clasped onto his arm and started to engage him in conversation. The vicar smiled and seemed genuinely pleased to be in her company. This did not go unnoticed by either Penny or Katie.

'Watch out for the fireworks,' she whispered in her husband's ear. By moving her head subtly Penny managed to explain to Steve what she was alluding to.

Katie Robertson glared at Sam Crouch as she and the vicar sat together in the corner. It was clear to Katie that the hairdresser had the full attention of the vicar, who had not even acknowledged her existence.

Meanwhile, Sam Crouch was totally captivated by the conversation. It looked to Penny that she may have stolen a march over her rival for the vicar's attention.

'One nil to Sam,' said Penny in an almost muted voice.

'Maybe not,' replied her astonished husband, who had the benefit of seeing someone enter the bar over his wife's shoulder.

'The drinks are on me, landlord,' shouted the man in the doorway.

To the surprise of most of the occupants of the bar, but especially Penny, Katie and Sam, it was Barney Green who had just entered the bar. In almost perfect unison the three women did a double take.

'So who is that man with Sam?' Penny asked Steve.

'I don't know,' he replied, 'but it must be his twin. They are so alike.'

As Barney made his way to the bar, he was roaring with laughter. 'It's a little game we have played since we were kids,' he said to Steve and Penny. 'Let me introduce you all to my twin brother, Bartholomew. He's a vicar too, you know.'

Penny watched the faces of Sam and Katie to see their reaction. Katie was clearly relieved, and her mood improved even more when Barney made a bee-line for where she was standing. Sam Crouch, on the other hand, at first looked stunned. However, as Bartholomew quietly explained to her what was going on, Penny could see that Sam's attitude quickly improved.

'One, one,' commented Steve, who, to Penny's astonishment, had also been observing the body language of the two ladies.

Marc Watson rolled into the station that Sunday morning at a little after eleven. Had he managed to make it to the station earlier, he and Paul Cooper would probably have already been at Bradley Monroe's house when Carl Tanner arrived. For certain Tanner would not have attempted to enter the property knowing that two police officers were there. However, Watson did not arrive at the station as early as his colleague, and the two officers only managed to arrive at Bradley Monroe's house at 12.15. Carl Tanner had already entered the house by then. Tanner made his entrance in his normal manner, by making a small hole in the window of the back door, which he then used to help him unlock the door from the inside. Once safely indoors he carefully started to look around for money and valuables. He had learned only to take items that were easily portable. He had no use for anything larger as he wanted to be able to leave just as quietly and unobtrusively as he had arrived, and he had found it very hard to get any real value from larger items. Cash and jewellery were his prime targets.

Watson and Cooper had almost reached the front door when Tanner quietly slid into Monroe's front room. There could not have been more than a second between the door bell ringing and Tanner seeing the body of Bradley Monroe slumped in the chair, his mouth and eyes wide open, and dried blood caked on the side of his face and shirt.

Tanner panicked. He ran back into the kitchen. Within half a minute he was out of the house and, without looking back, ran towards the fence at the back of the garden. Had he elected to hide rather than clamber over the 6-foot wooden fence, it is likely that Cooper would not have noticed him. However, in his state of fear, Tanner was not thinking properly. Being slightly built and having strong arms, he was able to haul himself up and was halfway over the fence when Cooper's massive hands clamped hold of his leg and pulled him back down into the garden he had been fleeing.

Although they were identical in appearance, had a similar sense of humour and had both chosen the same vocation, Barney and Bart

Green were very different in character. Barney had always liked the limelight and was totally gregarious; his brother was much quieter and more reserved. Barney was the one who had always been popular at school and had many acquaintances, while Bart had only a small circle of very close friends. In spite of their obvious differences the brothers had always got on well.

Once the shock of what had happened in the pub had subsided, the guests in the Railway resumed their conversations. To Katie's delight Barney Green remained at the bar, and although he spent some time in pleasant conversation with those who stood near him, his main focus of attention was clearly on the pretty young barmaid who smiled back at him at every opportunity. The mutual attention was not lost on Robbie Robertson, who still had no idea that the two had already been seeing each other. Sam Crouch did not notice any of the goings on at the bar as she was far too preoccupied with Bart Green, who was as handsome as his brother, but much more attentive.

By the time Carmichael received the call from Watson he had already drunk too much to be able to drive. 'Can you call me a taxi?' he said to Katie Robertson.

'What's the matter?' enquired Penny.

'That was Watson,' Steve replied in a hushed voice. 'They've found the body of Lillia Monroe's husband at his house.'

'Oh my God!' exclaimed Penny. 'Was he murdered too?'

Steve shrugged his shoulders. 'I don't know, but from what Watson was saying it certainly looks that way.'

It took no more than five minutes for the taxi to arrive.

'Do you want to be dropped off at home?' Steve asked.

'Er, no,' replied Penny with a glint in her eye. 'I'll stay here for a while. I think I'll go and sit with Sam and Barney's brother. They seem to be getting on like a house on fire.' With that she kissed her husband on the cheek and sauntered off in the direction of her quarry. Steve watched her walk over and then made his exit from the Railway Tavern.

Chapter 21

It took no more than fifteen minutes for the taxi to arrive at Bradley Monroe's house. The scene of crime officers had been called but had not yet arrived, so when Steve walked up the path only Watson and two uniformed officers were in attendance.

'Where's Cooper?' Carmichael asked impatiently.

'He went back to the station with the burglar,' replied Watson.

Carmichael nodded and walked passed Watson and in through Monroe's front door.

'He's through there,' said Watson pointing into the lounge.

Carmichael walked into the room and over to the body. 'Has anybody touched him?' he asked.

'Cooper felt for a pulse,' replied Watson, 'but he said that the body was stone cold. My guess is that he has been dead a while.'

'After my job, Sergeant?' boomed Dr Stock, as he made his entrance. 'I did not know that you were a qualified pathologist.'

'Afternoon, Dr Stock,' said Carmichael. 'I think even we mere mortals can see that he's been dead a little while, and that he was probably killed by a blow to the side of the head.' As he spoke Carmichael pointed down to the blood-stained wine bottle that lay on its side next to the chair. 'But we will leave it to your expertise to corroborate this and to hopefully give us a little more detail about the manner and timing of Bradley Monroe's demise.'

'You know the victim then?' Stock asked.

'Yes,' replied Carmichael, 'he's the husband of the woman found in Harper's Lake. To be honest, even though he had a very strong alibi for the time of that murder, I still had a gut feeling that he was involved. The last thing I expected was for him to be killed too and in such a similar way.'

'I guess we can cross him off our list of suspects,' said Watson.

'Yes,' agreed Carmichael. 'I think Bradley can officially be removed from our list of prime suspects for Lillia's death. The question is who on earth would have a motive to kill Lillia *and* Bradley?'

Carmichael decided not to stay too long at the crime scene. He didn't feel that his presence was necessary and, after consuming three or four pints that lunchtime, he did not feel in the right frame of mind to do any police work that afternoon. Having been in the house for less than an hour, he left Watson, Stock and the SOCOs and made his way home in the back of PC Tyler's police car. On the way back he called Cooper at the station to find out how he was getting on with interviewing Carl Tanner, the burglar.

'He's confessing to pretty much all the unsolved break-ins,' Cooper announced. 'But he's denying any involvement in Monroe's murder.'

'That's great,' replied Carmichael, as the police car arrived at his house. 'Hewitt will be delirious with joy when he learns that we have cleared up all our pending burglaries, well done.'

Cooper laughed. 'The Chief Inspector may not be quite so happy when he learns how Tanner managed to carry out so many burglaries without being detected. You just will not believe it.'

Steve was still laughing at what Cooper had just told him as he turned the key of his front door.

It was another hour before Penny arrived home. She had spent most of the last two hours in deep conversation with Sam Crouch and Bartholomew Green in the Railway Tavern. At first she did not realise that Steve was already at home. It was only when she made herself a mug of coffee and walked into the lounge that she noticed him, seemingly dead to the world but breathing loudly, in his favourite armchair.

As Penny sat down, Jemma entered the room. 'Can I borrow thirty pounds, please?' she asked her mother. 'I'm going out to-night and I didn't have a chance to get to the cash point today.'

'Fetch my purse,' Penny sighed as she pointed towards the door. 'It's in my bag in the kitchen.'

Jemma walked out of the room, closing the door behind her. The loud thud of the door as it shut jolted Steve back to life.

'Oh, hello,' said Penny. 'Did you have a nice nap?'

Steve rubbed his eyes. 'What time is it?' he asked.

'It's about four-thirty,' she replied. 'How did you get on at the Monroes' house?'

'I didn't stay long,' he yawned. 'Marc and Dr Stock seemed to have everything under control, so I left them to it.'

'Was it murder?' asked Penny.

'Oh yes, I'm sure of that,' Steve replied. 'And it was probably committed by the same person who killed his wife.'

Jemma re-entered the lounge. 'Here you are,' she said as she passed her mother's purse to her. Penny pulled out three ten pound notes and handed them to her daughter. 'I want paying back,' she said sternly.

Jemma gave her mother a kiss on the cheek. 'I'll pay you back tomorrow,' she said with a smile, just as soon as I can get to the cash point.' With that she left the room and headed towards her bedroom.

'Do you have any ideas about who the murderer might be?' Penny enquired.

'To be truthful, no,' he replied. 'This latest murder has really thrown a spanner in the works. Up until now I had assumed that Lillia's murderer was likely to have been someone she had upset. Perhaps a jilted lover, or maybe a jealous rival, and if she was earning money as an escort then I had thought that it may have been one of her clients. Bradley Monroe's death, if it is connected to Lillia's, which it must be, is not consistent with any of these theories.'

'I see,' said Penny thoughtfully. 'What if

Lillia was an escort, but rather than being oblivious to the fact, what if her husband knew and was a willing accomplice? Maybe they could have double-crossed someone who has now killed them both out of revenge. Or maybe they have been killed by some other rival escort agency.'

Steve smiled. 'These are all possibilities, I suppose, but I'd be surprised if they were working together like that. I'm also still not sure she was an escort.'

'So what's your plan, Sherlock?' Penny asked as she sat on his lap.

'For this afternoon to just try and get some time away from work,' he replied with another yawn. 'As for tomorrow, I intend to spend most of the day reading the translation of Lillia's diary. That will have all the answers, I'm certain.'

Chapter 22

Rachel's date with Gregor Padar on Saturday evening had gone well. She thought he was incredibly good-looking and found him very charming. Without any hesitation she had agreed to meet him again for lunch the following day.

When Rachel reached their agreed meeting place at the Drunken Duck, a picturesque and remote country pub tucked away in the small hamlet of Small Heath, her date had already arrived and was seated in a quiet corner of the room, sipping a Diet Coke. Next to him was a large folder stuffed with his typed translation of Lillia Monroe's diary.

'Hello, Gregor,' she said as she sat down next to him. 'Is that the English translation of the diary?'

'Yes,' replied Gregor in his thick Eastern European accent. 'It's not everything, I have done about sixty or seventy per cent, but I will work late this evening so that your boss has it all by the morning as I promised.'

Rachel and Gregor spent the next two hours immersed in each other's company, during which time Rachel took the opportunity to read through some of the diary that her handsome new boyfriend had already translated.

'This is unbelievable,' she kept saying. 'I can't wait to see what Inspector Carmichael makes of this.'

'She was an interesting lady,' said Gregor,

as Rachel finally put down the manuscript.

'You can say that again,' said Rachel. 'Can you leave this with me, as I'd like to read it all through this evening?'

'Of course,' confirmed Gregor. 'That is why I brought it with me. But maybe we can talk about something else while we are together.'

Rachel carefully placed the translation back in its folder and placed the folder next to her.

'You have my full attention,' she said as she stared into his dark brown eyes.

Carmichael arrived at the station at 7:30 the next morning. He parked his car next to Chief Inspector Hewitt's and strode purposefully into the station. For once he was really looking forward to his briefing with the boss. He was particularly keen to divulge to Hewitt that the serial burglar had been caught. He could not wait to see the look on Hewitt's face when he revealed how the burglar had managed to carry out five successful break-ins in broad daylight without being detected.

It was not unusual for Hewitt to arrive at the station before Steve, however, Steve was surprised to find Rachel Dalton at her desk when he arrived.

'Morning Rachel,' he said as he walked over towards his office. 'You're in bright and early.'

'Morning, sir,' replied Rachel, who could not contain her excitement. 'I have most of the translated diary, sir,' she said. 'I've been reading through it and it's really interesting.'

Carmichael walked back to Rachel's desk. 'Your translator friend is hot off the mark. Did he deliver it this morning?'

'Well, actually, no,' Rachel spluttered. 'I met him yesterday and he gave me what he had already completed. He promises to bring the rest over this morning.'

'I see,' Carmichael said. 'And am I to assume that your meeting with him yesterday was just on police business, or is there a bit more to it than that?'

Rachel was now blushing heavily. 'We had lunch together yesterday,' she quietly confessed. 'He gave me all the translations that he'd done so far, but yes, I have agreed to see him again if that's what you are asking.'

'Look, Rachel,' said Carmichael firmly. 'There's nothing that says that you can't date people, but please be careful what you say to your new young man. Your relationship with him is your own business, but you

208

need to make sure that you do not discuss the case with him. That's strictly police business.'

'I understand,' replied Rachel.

'Good,' said Carmichael. 'Anyway what have you discovered about Lillia?' Rachel was just about to start her summary of what she had read in the diary, when Cooper and Watson arrived.

'Morning, guys,' shouted Carmichael. 'Get yourselves over here. Rachel's done some good work looking at the translation of the diary. She was just about to enlighten me.' Carmichael signalled to Rachel to start her summary.

'Well,' said Rachel. 'It would appear that Lillia was not quite what we thought.'

'Don't tell me,' said Watson flippantly. 'She was a KGB secret agent, who was working under cover as a high-class prostitute.'

'No,' replied Rachel. 'Lillia was an Estonian, as we know, born Lillia Kruglov in Paldiski near Tallin. She was a quarter Russian due to her maternal grandfather being a Russian soldier, but I think that was as far as any KGB connections went. On her twenty-first birthday she was given the ten-year diary and also the Russian Orthodox cross, which thereafter she almost always wore.'

'We never did find that cross, did we?' Carmichael declared. 'I wonder where it is?'

Rachel paused briefly before continuing with her findings. 'This was almost six years ago. In the front of the diary someone had written a message that said something along the lines of: *To achieve greatness a woman must use all her skills, her looks, her powers of persuasion but above all her intellect.* Judging from what I have read so far this is a motto that Lillia was to follow with a passion.'

The three men sat attentively as Rachel continued. 'At the time she received the diary, she was working as an English translator at a small factory in Tallin that appears to have made self-assembly furniture, the sort of stuff you buy from do-it-yourself stores. She had a boyfriend called Jany, who she had been dating since she was at school, and she lived at home with her mother and father. For the first year or so her entries were interesting but very mundane. Apart from Jany her main interest at that time appears to be her horse. It looks as though she was a good horsewoman and often won horse-jumping competitions in Estonia.' Steve thought back to his conversations with Hannah De Vere. She had indicated that Lillia was a good rider. He said nothing though, as he was keen for Rachel to carry on.

'However, unfortunately for Lillia,' continued Rachel, 'when she turned twenty-two, both her parents died in fairly short succession. Her father died in a freak accident at work. Then, about six months later, her mother contracted some form of virus that seems to have taken hold quickly and within a few weeks of being diagnosed, she had also died.'

'Poor girl,' said Cooper with genuine sympathy.

'Yes, but importantly this appears to have been some sort of watershed for Lillia,' said Rachel. 'Her writing after that changes dramatically. Almost as soon as her mother dies, her entries start to become different, almost neurotic. She no longer talks about the normal things women note down in their diaries, now she is almost totally preoccupied with bettering herself. Just about every other entry from then on talks about how she needs to become wealthy and acquire influence and power. She appears to be obsessed with finding ways to reach her goal.'

'What sort of things does she say?' Carmichael asked.

'Well, as an example,' replied Rachel, 'in her entry dated twenty-first July 2002, she talks about her then boss asking her to go out for a drink the following evening. I don't know how old this man was, but in her entry she writes:

"He really is a most unattractive man. He is old, fat, vain and is not at all good at his job. However, he will be able to help me get the sales job that is being advertised, so I have no problem in just having a few nights out with him. If it helps me get what I want then I can put up with a little inconvenience."

'That's women for you, Paul,' Watson whispered to Cooper. 'You just can't trust them.'

'Shh, Marc,' snapped Carmichael. 'Continue, Rachel.'

'Well, she goes out with him a few times and within the month she has the sales job,' announced Rachel. 'Once she gets that job she does not seem to have much more to do with her boss. Also, a few weeks after getting the job she ditches Jany because, as she puts it, *he has no ambition.* Then she starts applying for sales jobs in America and in Britain. She appears to believe that her chances of bettering herself and growing wealthy are going to be greater if she lives either here or in America.'

'Was she successful?' Carmichael asked.

'It would appear not,' replied Rachel. 'Much to her disgust, she does not appear to be have even been given an interview.'

'So what does she do then?' asked Cooper.

'She hits upon the idea of marrying an American or an Englishman as she realises that by doing so she could gain citizenship.'

'And her entry into the promised land,' interrupted Carmichael.

'Yes,' confirmed Rachel. 'That's almost exactly how she puts it in her diary.'

'So was her marriage to Monroe just a way of getting British citizenship?' asked Watson.

'I think so,' said Rachel. 'However, it's clear she did find him attractive and I did not see many entries about him that were that critical. She found him a bit possessive and a little weak at times, but from what I read I'd say she was fond of him.'

'Do you think he knew about her diary and her obsession for wealth and power?' Carmichael asked.

'I couldn't say,' replied Rachel. 'I don't think he knew what sort of things she was up to, but from her entries in her diary it's not that clear.'

'Monroe did tell us that he met Lillia when he was working out there for a short while,' said Watson.

'So let me get this right,' said Carmichael. 'She finds her English man. He's fairly attractive to her so she marries him and comes back to live in the UK. What then?'

'She finds a good friend in Hannah De Vere,' replied Rachel. 'She calls her Lady Di, which was her way of paying Hannah a compliment. I think Hannah was her only real friend in this country. From her entries in her diary, Lillia clearly admired Hannah and certainly aspired to one day have the wealth and social standing that her friend enjoyed.'

'What about the other nicknames? Did the diary reveal who they were?' asked Watson.

'Other than Lady Di, the only ones revealed in what I've read were PM, which is Peter Monroe, who I assume is Bradley's brother. She mentions him now and then, and she appears to have quite liked him, but he was not in the diary much. Also I discovered that TF stands for Tom Fool, which was her less than flattering nickname for Tom Sharwood.'

At the mention of Sharwood Carmichael

became more interested. 'What does she say about TF then?'

'He started to be mentioned towards the end of the translations that I read. She met him at the rugby club quite soon after she and Bradley got married. He appears to have taken a shine to her and initially she plays him along. The translation that I read only went up to about two years ago, but at that time Lillia was looking for a job in sales or finance. She appears to have identified Sharwood as her way to get a job at Gemini. Unknown to Bradley she sees Sharwood for drinks a few times, but in her diary entries she has nothing but disparaging comments about him.'

'Like what?' Cooper asked.

'Well on March twenty-sixth 2005, which was one of the last entries that has been translated, she wrote:

"Had a secret drink with TF. It was a cool evening but I still wore my cotton dress. He could not keep his eyes off me and started making promises of work at Gemini. He clearly adores me and I am sure that I'll soon be working at Gemini. The sooner that happens the better as he is so boring and I can't wait to dump him."

'So, what is your take on Lillia, now you've read four years of her diary entries?' asked Carmichael.

Rachel thought for a moment. 'She was smart, she was calculating, she certainly did not feel afraid of using her looks to gain advantage, but I'd say she was quite lonely and sad.'

'Do you think that she was a paid escort?' Carmichael enquired.

Rachel gave this question careful thought. 'There is no evidence of that in the extracts that I read,' she stated. 'And my hunch would be that she was not working as an escort, but whether she would actually sleep with men if it got her what she wanted is more difficult to judge. There was no evidence of her doing this so far in the diary entries I read, but maybe she did later with Sharwood and I'm not so sure that Ralf Marsh was telling us the truth when he said that he wasn't paying her.'

'Well, as soon as your translator arrives with the rest of the diary in English we may finally get some answers to these questions,' said Carmichael. 'Until then I'd like to review where we are on this one.'

'Shall I update our three charts?' asked Watson.

'Yes,' replied Carmichael, 'but this time I want to add a fourth list. This one is for possible suspects for either or both murders.'

It took the four officers about forty minutes to review the case and create a list of suspects to add to their three other lists.
The list they compiled was short, with just four names:

1. Ralph Marsh
2. Tom Sharwood
3. Allison Marsh
4. Ruth Andrews

Carmichael surveyed the various lists. 'Who should be our prime suspect?' he asked the team.
'I don't think any are very strong,' said Cooper. 'However, I'd say Ruth Andrews is someone who we should consider, certainly for Lillia's death.'
'Maybe,' replied Carmichael, 'but we have no evidence she even knew Bradley, so why would she kill him?'
'I think that Sharwood has got to be our prime suspect,' said Watson. 'He was clearly infatuated by Lillia, he knew Bradley, which the others didn't, and I would have thought

that had he found out that Lillia was sleeping with Marsh he would have been very jealous.'

'You may be right,' said Rachel, 'but all I can say is that Allison Marsh has a nasty temper and if pushed into a corner I think she could commit murder.'

'In truth none are that strong as suspects,' said Carmichael with a sigh, 'but I have to side with Marc and say that if I had to pick one it would be Sharwood. He's clearly the one who seems to be the most likely killer.'

'Do you want us to pick him up?' asked Cooper.

Carmichael thought for a moment. 'I certainly think we need to interview him and Ruth Andrews again, but until we get the estimated time of death for our second murder from Dr Stock, I think we should keep our powder dry. Also, I want to read the rest of Lillia's diary before we make our next move.'

Chapter 23

Hewitt was frozen in shock and horror. His mouth gaped open and what little colour he normally had in his thin face drained away completely. For almost a full minute he remained motionless in his chair, his eyes transfixed and unblinking.

'Let me get this straight,' he said slowly and deliberately. 'The man who has been breaking into houses in the outlying villages is called Carl Tanner.'

'That's right,' replied Carmichael.

'And you are telling me that he is employed by Lancashire Police as a Community Policeman,' continued the Chief Inspector.

Carmichael tried desperately not to laugh or show any sign of pleasure or amusement. 'That's about it.'

Hewitt fidgeted nervously with the expensive silver pen on his desk. 'And you say Cooper and Watson caught him red-handed and he has confessed to all the burglaries?'

'Correct,' said Carmichael, who could feel the sides of his mouth lifting to display a smile, 'every single one.'

'This will be all over the local papers, on the local radio and on TV,' said Hewitt, his stare fixed at the desk in front of him. 'It's a PR disaster!'

'I suspect it may even make the nationals,' interrupted Carmichael with a hint of glee.

Hewitt picked up the telephone. 'Can you get hold of the Deputy Chief Constable for me please, Angela?'

Steve waited a few moments. The chief was in such a state of shock that he no longer realised that Carmichael was there.

'If it's OK with you, sir, I'd like to get on with the Lillia Monroe case,' Steve said, his message now fully delivered. Hewitt indicated that he could go, and Steve quickly left his boss in his moment of grief.

As Carmichael was leaving the room, he heard Hewitt on the phone to the Deputy Chief Constable in Preston.

'Good morning sir,' he said in a shaky voice. 'I'm afraid I've some bad news regarding one of our Community Police Officers.'

Steve closed the door behind him and triumphantly marched down the corridor beaming from ear to ear.

Penny's morning had started like most

mornings that summer, with her first task being to make sure that Robbie was up and out for work on time, before getting herself ready to take Natalie to the stables. Jemma was still in bed. Having not got back home the evening before until after midnight, which was fast becoming her routine, Penny knew that Jemma was unlikely to rise until at least late morning, and quite possibly not even until lunch was over.

It was just after 9 am when Penny and Natalie arrived at the stables. Hannah De Vere and Stan Foster were in deep conversation at the side of the stable block, hidden away from the house. They were standing very close together and although Penny was not sure, it looked very much like the palm of Stan's right hand was gently resting upon Hannah's bottom. At first they did not notice Penny's car arrive, but once they did they moved apart quickly like naughty school children caught cuddling behind the bike sheds.

'Hannah,' Penny shouted through the open window of the car. 'Have you got a minute?'

True to his word, Gregor Padar delivered the translated manuscript to the station that morning.

'I hope that it helps,' he said to Rachel as he handed it over to her in the main entrance hall.

'Thank you, Gregor,' replied Rachel with a smile.

'Do you want to go out again some time?' he asked.

Embarrassed that they may be overheard Rachel gently whispered, 'Yes that would be great, I'll call you tonight.'

Without any warning, Gregor bent down and gave Rachel a peck on her cheek before he left the station.

Rachel's fear of being observed was well placed. She knew full well that, should her colleagues realise she was seeing Gregor, she would instantly become the main subject of conversation at the station and she was keen to keep this new relationship a secret. She was especially keen to make sure Marc Watson did not find out, as she knew that he would make her life a misery with his incessant childish taunts, if he knew.

Sadly for Rachel her worst fears were to become a reality. Marc Watson had observed everything. Having parked up his car directly in front of the station doorway just as the translator arrived, he had witnessed the whole of Rachel and Gregor's meeting. He waited for Rachel to go out of the foyer before he smugly clambered out of his car and with a spring in his step, strode hurriedly into the station.

When Carmichael finally arrived back in the office, Watson, Cooper and Dalton were all quietly reading through the translated pages of Lillia's diary that Gregor had delivered earlier.

'Here's your copy, sir,' said Rachel, when she saw her boss enter the room. 'I made four photocopies so we could all read through the final pages.'

'Thanks,' said Carmichael as he grabbed his copy and walked into his office. As he turned to close the door behind him, he shouted back at Rachel. 'Bring me the rest of the translated pages too.' Although he had been impressed by Rachel's earlier synopsis of the beginning of the diary, he wanted to make sure that she had not missed anything important in her summary, so he decided it would be wise to read through all of the translation for himself before deciding upon what should be the team's next step.

Once Penny had concluded her conversation with Hannah De Vere, she climbed back into her car, clutching the scrap of paper with the address and telephone number that Stan Foster had given her.

She drove slowly down the driveway, pausing only when she reached the main road. Before she made the turning towards Moulton Bank she looked back down the drive through her rear view mirror. Hannah and Foster had resumed their previous positions, oblivious to the fact that their obvious closeness was being noted by Penny. From this evidence Penny concluded that the two were more than just friends, and as she drove down the road she wondered whether Charles De Vere had any idea how close his wife and his trainer had become.

Steve was a slow reader and it took him more than three hours to read through the completed translation. Unbeknown to him it was while he was carefully studying the transcript of Lillia's diary that the murderer struck for the third time.

Chapter 24

The diary answered most of the questions Carmichael had been asking himself about the beautiful young woman who had died so tragically less than ten days before. As Rachel had stated during her summary of the early pages, it painted a vivid picture of a person who was so driven in her mission to achieve wealth and social standing, that she would do almost anything to attain her goal. As he carefully read through the translated pages, Carmichael found himself concurring with all that Rachel had observed. To a degree Lillia's determination impressed Carmichael, given that this was still a young woman and also someone far from her native country. However, as he read, Carmichael became less and less respectful of Lillia. The way that she manipulated everyone she came into contact with, irrespective of who they were, left Steve feeling little but contempt.

Her use of nicknames and the way she created them also suggested to Steve that Lillia was just a cold, cynical and self-absorbed individual, who cared little for those that she had met in England. Only Hannah De Vere and Ralf Marsh (who she had nicknamed Lady Di and Alan Sugar) were cited with any fondness. As for her husband, he was, as Rachel had said, probably someone who Lillia liked, but he did not appear to be someone that she loved and admired. In fact, the few mentions of Peter Monroe, her husband's brother, were generally more complimentary than the references she made to Bradley.

Ruth Andrews (Mutton) and Tom Sharwood (Tom Fool or TF) were the ones who consistently received the most ferocious criticism. It was clear that Lillia despised them both. To her, Ruth Andrews was just a middle-aged woman who thought she was important in the running of Gemini, and in Sharwood her diary revealed that she saw a weak individual who craved a rekindling of his short relationship with Lillia, and as such he was someone whom she could very easily manipulate. Her diary revealed in detail and with great pride how, as a result of her power over Sharwood, she was able to operate a money-making venture of her own. This was a straightforward scam whereby Lillia would accept and agree overpayments to Gemini's

PR agency, which Sharwood would approve. In return Lillia would receive in cash a payment of twelve hundred pounds a month from the PR company. As recompense for his support in the swindle, Lillia paid Sharwood one hundred and fifty pounds every Friday in cash. This was one of the sums of money Steve had noticed when he had first read the diary. Carmichael's previous theory was wrong: these payments were not, as he had thought, money she received for services given, but payments she made to Sharwood for his part in the fiddle.

'I wonder what Ralf Marsh will think when he finds out his Financial Director and his mistress were ripping his company off to the tune of twelve hundred pounds a month?' thought Steve with more than a small degree of pleasure.

The translation also revealed a second con that Lillia was orchestrating. This one did not involve Gemini, it did however, explain the real reason for Lillia and Hannah De Vere falling out a few months earlier.

On her way back from the stables, Penny decided to call in to the hair salon to see Sam Crouch. She wanted to solicit Sam's help in organising a surprise she was planning for Steve.

Unusually, the salon was very quiet that morning, which gave the two ladies the opportunity to discuss Sam's new relationship as well as Penny's plan.

'So?' said Penny as she sat down, cup of coffee in hand.

'So what?' replied Sam, pretending not to understand the question.

'You know what I mean,' continued Penny. 'Any developments with you and Bart Green?'

Sam leant forward with a broad smile on her face. 'He's invited me down to stay with him, although we have not agreed when.'

'That's quick work,' replied Penny. 'You don't let the grass grow, do you?'

Sam beamed from ear to ear. 'He's really cute. I think I'm in love.'

Penny smiled and shook her head. 'Don't you think you should take a little more time to get to know him? After all, less than a week ago you were head over heels in love with his brother.'

Sam laughed. 'Don't worry, I'm not about to do anything stupid, but I really do like him.'

Penny was just about to tell Sam about her surprise for Steve when a customer entered the salon.

'Hello Mrs Hornby,' Sam said with another bright smile. 'Take a seat, I'll be with you in a moment.' Sam turned back to face Penny. 'I'm going to have to leave you, Penny,' she said. 'The junior called in sick so I'm going to have to wash Mrs Hornby's hair.'

'That's fine,' replied Penny. 'I do need to talk to you though. I'm planning a surprise for Steve and I'd like your help.'

'What sort of surprise?' Sam asked with interest.

'Call me when you're free and I'll explain,' said Penny. 'I'm in all afternoon.'

'Ok, I'll call you later,' replied Sam. 'Actually I've got some spicy gossip to share with you too.'

'What's that?' Penny asked.

'I'll give you all the juicy details later,' she replied with a smirk on her face. 'All I will say now is that it involves some furtive goings on at Hardthorpe Manor.'

Penny left the salon and crossed the road towards her car. Sam Crouch watched her as she walked away, then she turned to attend to her next customer. 'My word, what a beautiful necklace you are wearing.'

Her customer smiled with pride. 'Yes my son gave it to me for my birthday.'

'OK, everyone,' said Carmichael. 'Now that we have all had time to read the transcript of Lillia's diary, let's take a few minutes to assess where we are.'

'Well, it's now clear that the amounts Lillia was recording in her diary were not payments she was receiving as we had thought, but they are sums she was paying out,' said Cooper.

'Yes, and it's also pretty evident that she was not an escort,' said Rachel.

'That's true,' commented Watson. 'But there is no doubt that she has been gaining much in the last few years by making use of her looks and through leading on her many admirers.'

'That does not make her a prostitute,' snapped Rachel angrily.

'Absolutely right,' said Carmichael calmly. 'But let's not kid ourselves here. Lillia knew that she was attractive to men and skilfully used this power at every opportunity to enhance her career, her personal wealth and her status.'

Realising her earlier outburst may have been an overreaction, Rachel smiled at Carmichael and gently nodded to illustrate her agreement.

'That being the case,' said Cooper, 'who are our main suspects now?' The four officers remained silent for a few moments.

'I still think we need to consider Ralf Marsh,' said Watson.

'Why do you say that?' asked Carmichael

'Well, he was having an affair with her and maybe she wanted to finish it,' he continued. 'We only have his word that they were still seeing each other.'

'I don't wear that,' interrupted Rachel. 'We know they were at the Lindley the Wednesday before Lillia's death, and Marsh booked the room for their next Wednesday liaison after Lillia had been killed. He only cancelled it on the Wednesday morning, which shows that he only knew about her death when Ruth Andrews told him. That was after Inspector Carmichael and Cooper went to Gemini.'

'I have the same opinion,' said Cooper. 'He must be a suspect but I'm not convinced he's our man. I think Ruth Andrews is more likely. She hated Lillia and her alibi for the Saturday that Lillia died is very weak.'

'Maybe,' said Rachel, 'but we don't know of any reason for her to kill Bradley Monroe.'

'That's a fair point,' agreed Cooper.

'What do you think, sir?' asked Watson.

'Well,' said Carmichael. 'I can only think of one potential candidate who may have killed them both and that is Tom Sharwood. He's the only one who knew both Lillia and Bradley that well. He was clearly in love with Lillia, although she was not interested, and if the diary is correct he was up to his neck with her in the fraud with the PR agency, but as it stands I'm not sure we have anywhere near enough evidence to make an arrest.'

'So what's the plan?' asked Cooper.

'Marc and I will get ourselves over to Gemini and have another chat with Sharwood about the fraud. In the meantime I'd like you, Paul, to track down Bradley's brother, Peter. We will need someone to do the formal identification of the body, so he should do that. However, more importantly, I'm keen to find out a little more from him about Bradley and Lillia's relationship.'

'From reading the diary,' interrupted Watson, 'we probably also need to find out if there was any relationship going on between Peter and Lillia too.'

'You're right,' said Carmichael. 'She did tend to mention him fondly whenever he made it into the diary.' Cooper nodded and left the room to take up his assignment.

'What would you like me to do?' asked Rachel.

'Get hold of Lillia's bank statements,' replied Carmichael. 'Her diary mentions two scams. I want to see the money trail on these and I'd also like to know if she was up to any other little money making rackets.'

'That's fine,' replied Rachel, who followed Cooper out of the office.

'What about the other con?' asked Watson. 'Don't you think one of us should be following that up too?'

Carmichael smiled. 'I don't think that particular fiddle is connected to the murders,' he said. 'Let's see how we get on with Sharwood first. The other scam will keep until later.'

Chapter 25

'How do you want to play this?' Watson asked Carmichael as they drove to Gemini.

'I think we should keep our main line of questioning on the fraud,' suggested Carmichael. 'Let's see how that develops first and take it from there.'

'Do we inform Marsh about it?' Watson asked.

'If we are going to prove this we will need to get copies of the invoices raised and payments made,' replied Carmichael. 'That being the case I think we will need the help of either Marsh or Ruth Andrews, but let's make sure there is some truth in what Lillia put in her diary first before we leap ahead of ourselves.'

'I agree,' said Watson. 'And there's always the chance that Marsh or Andrews are in on the scam too.'

Carmichael nodded in agreement. 'Good point Marc, I had not thought of that scenario.'

Cooper and Rachel decided to go back to Lillia and Bradley's home. When they arrived the house was still cordoned off with an officer on guard.

'We need to make sure we don't disturb things,' said Cooper as they arrived. 'Once we've found what we are looking for we need to be out of there.'

'OK,' replied Rachel. 'It shouldn't take me long to find details of Lillia's bank accounts, but if I can't, I guess I can get her bank details from Ruth Andrews at Gemini.'

Cooper nodded in agreement 'Let's hope it's as easy for me to find an address or telephone number of Peter Monroe,' he said.

Penny called the number that Stan Foster had written down for her that morning.

'Oh, good morning,' she said. 'I would like to enquire about a booking for Saturday the twenty-fourth of August and also the cost of race sponsorship.'

'Certainly,' replied the voice at the end of the line. 'I'll put you through to our commercial manager's office.'

It was just after 2 pm when Carmichael and Watson arrived at Gemini.

'OK, Marc,' said Carmichael. 'Let's see what Mr Sharwood has to say for himself.' The two officers walked into the reception area and, having identified themselves to the young girl behind the desk, asked to see Tom Sharwood.

'I haven't seen him today,' replied the receptionist. 'I'll try his number.'

When she received no reply, she dialled Ruth Andrews. 'Oh, hello, it's Amy here. I've got two police officers in reception to see Mr Sharwood, but I'm not getting any reply from his number.'

After a short pause the receptionist put down the phone. 'Ruth will be down in a moment,' she replied. 'Please take a seat.'

It took Ruth Andrews only a few moments to enter reception. 'Hello, gentlemen,' she said. 'I'm afraid Tom's not come in yet. We did expect him but so far we've not heard from him and he's not answering his mobile or his home telephone.'

Carmichael and Watson exchanged a look. 'Can you give us Mr Sharwood's address?' said Carmichael. 'We need to speak to him urgently.'

'Of course,' replied Andrews. 'He lives in Newbridge. It's number five Albury Gardens.'

'Thank you,' said Carmichael. 'If he does turn up or if you do manage to speak to him, can you ask Mr Sharwood to call me at the station?'

'Of course,' replied Ruth Andrews.

'Before we go,' continued Carmichael. 'Can we have a brief chat with Mr Marsh?'

Ruth Andrews shook her head. 'I'm afraid Mr Marsh isn't in today either. His wife called in this morning to say that he was not feeling well. Apparently he fell down some stairs at the weekend and has a nasty cut and is suffering from slight concussion.'

Carmichael tried to look surprised. 'Oh, I am sorry to hear that,' he said. 'I do hope he gets well soon.'

Sam Crouch tried several times to call Penny that afternoon.

However on each occasion she rang she was greeted with the engaged tone. It was almost 3 pm when she finally managed to get through.

'You've been busy,' she said.

Penny laughed. 'Yes, I've been calling around trying to sort out this surprise for Steve for our twentieth wedding anniversary.'

'Oh, that's nice,' replied Sam. 'What are you planning?'

'I've booked a private room at the race track and have sponsored one of the races,' she exclaimed. 'It wasn't that expensive and, of course, you and Bart are invited.'

'Sounds great, thank you,' replied Sam. 'So how many other people are you inviting?'

'I've booked for twenty people,' Penny replied. 'I've called around a few of Steve's closest colleagues at work to come with their partners and I've invited Robbie Robertson and Katie from the pub. Katie's bringing

Barney and I've also asked Hannah De Vere and Charles to come too.'

'Oh really,' said Sam. 'Did they all accept?'

'Well, so far all except for Charles,' replied Penny. 'Hannah said she would come, but was not so sure about her husband's availability.'

'Umm,' said Sam knowingly. 'That sort of neatly falls in line with the bit of gossip that I mentioned earlier.'

'Really?' said Penny expectantly. 'What gossip is that then?'

It took Rachel only a few minutes to find the drawer where Lillia Monroe kept her bank statements and old cheque book stubs.

'Blimey,' she shrieked as she read through the statements. 'Look at all this, Cooper.' Cooper gently leaned over his colleague's shoulder and started to read the entries in the statement.

'Wow,' he said. 'So, let me get this right, she was taking home one thousand four hundred pounds a month from her job at Gemini, but most months she was getting payments from on-line betting companies into her account of almost double her salary.'

'Correct,' replied Rachel. 'Also, other than a few standing orders and direct debits for bills and payments into her deposit account, there are almost no withdrawals. So what did she do for spending money?'

'Good point,' replied Cooper. 'She probably used the cash she got from the PR company scam for that.'

'I'll get onto the betting companies and get some statements on the races she was betting on,' said Rachel. 'But from what she wrote in her diary, I think we both have a good idea how she was winning.'

'I'd also check out this regular payment she was making,' said Cooper, pointing to a five hundred pound standing order that was being paid to the same account every other week. 'I suspect that will nail at least one of her co-conspirators.'

Albury Gardens was a small and quiet cul-de-sac of just nine houses, which backed onto Newbridge village cricket pitch.

'Nice house,' observed Watson as they pulled up outside. 'It certainly looks like our Mr Sharwood was doing all right for himself.'

'Yes,' Carmichael concurred. 'I suspect that someone in his position was earning a pretty good salary. Which does beg the question, why would he need to be part of a fiddle with Lillia which earned him only a hundred and fifty pounds a week?'

Watson pondered this question for a moment. 'I don't know,' he replied. 'I think some people may do these things just because they think they can get away with it.'

'Maybe,' Carmichael said. 'Or what's more likely, is that it kept his relationship with Lillia alive. If he was as obsessed with her as she makes out in her diary, maybe it was simply the thought of being involved with her in all this which was his motivation.'

'Well, we should find out in the next few minutes,' announced Watson. 'That's unless he's done a runner.'

Carmichael opened the wrought iron gate, which creaked as he pushed it back. The two officers walked leisurely along the concrete path and up to the front door. To their surprise the door was slightly ajar. Carmichael slowly pushed it open and shouted down the corridor. 'Mr Sharwood, it's the police, can we come in?'

When they received no answer, Watson repeated the question but a good deal louder.

'You check upstairs, Marc,' said Carmichael. 'I'll take a look down here.'

Watson slowly ascended the staircase and stepped onto the landing. Carmichael gently pushed open the door to Sharwood's front room and peered in. 'Watson,' he shouted. 'He's in here.'

Within the space of half an hour the small house had been cordoned off and Dr Stock had arrived.

'That's three suspicious deaths in less than ten days. Only a few more to go and you'll have smashed your previous impressive record,' said Stock with a grin. Carmichael ignored the doctor's comments.

'Do you have any idea of the time of death?' he asked.

'Not a hundred per cent sure,' replied Stock. 'But I'd say fairly recent. He's certainly been dead for no more than five or six hours. My guess is that the time of death would have been at about ten o'clock this morning.' Steve was surprised that Stock was able and willing to be so precise.

'And the cause of death?' enquired Watson.

'Well, looking at the bruising around the face and the marks around his wrist, I'd guess that he was tied up and subjected to a severe beating, maybe over the space of an hour or two. But I'm also pretty sure that the cause of death was strangulation. I'll know for sure once I get him back to the lab and do the post mortem.'

Carmichael wandered outside and sat alone on a small bench at the back of the house. As he pondered this current development his mobile rang.

'Carmichael,' he said quietly.

Cooper's excited voice exploded from out of his handset. 'We've made good progress here. I thought I'd just update you.' Carmichael listened intently.

'That's great work,' he said. 'There have been a few developments here too.'

By the time Steve called Penny to tell her that he would be home late, she had already pretty much organised the whole of the surprise party for their wedding anniversary, and when he eventually arrived home Penny and the rest of the family were already asleep in their beds.

Chapter 26

'Just look at that rain,' remarked Steve as he peered out of the window. 'I hope Messrs De Vere and Foster both have their coats with them when they're picked up.'

'What do you mean?' asked Penny from under the duvet.

Steve looked at his watch. 'Well, in about an hour Charles De Vere and Stan Foster are due to be arrested and taken to the station. I'm planning to start interviewing De Vere at ten am with Rachel Dalton and at the same time Cooper and Watson will be interviewing Foster. That's, of course, assuming they have suitable legal representation.'

'On what charge are they being held?' asked Penny, who by now was sitting upright in bed.

'Fraud,' replied Steve. 'To be precise, race fixing. It appears to have been a little racket that they and Lillia were engaged in.'

'Race fixing!' exclaimed Penny. 'Surely not.'

'There's little doubt,' Steve confirmed. 'We have almost a confession from Lillia in her diary and, remember the sums of five hundred pounds that Lillia had against the person she coded Lap Dog? Well, it turns out that these correspond with standing order payments that she was making to Charles De Vere every two weeks. Unless he can explain these away then I think we have him banged to rights.'

'My God,' exclaimed Penny. 'But that does not implicate Stan Foster?'

'No, not directly,' replied Steve, 'but I can't see how Lillia and De Vere could have managed to carry out the fraud without Foster's help, as he's in charge of all of the dogs being bet on and these were all owned by Charles De Vere.'

Penny thought back to the conversation she had had the day before with Sam Crouch. 'Actually,' she said. 'There may be another explanation.'

'Oh really?' said Steve with interest. 'Do tell me more.'

Although he and Rachel had made great strides in finding out about Lillia's finances, Cooper had largely drawn a blank when it came to uncovering the whereabouts of Peter Monroe. The only lead that he had managed to find at Bradley and Lillia's house was an old school report for Bradley that he had found at the bottom of a drawer. His hope was that Peter Monroe had also attended the same school and that he might be able to locate him through the school's old boys network.

Knowing that he was due to start interviewing Stan Foster at 10 am, Cooper had arrived at the station early and was already busy making phone calls when the others started to arrive.

'Any joy, Paul?' Carmichael asked.

'I think it's fairly likely that the brothers went to the same school. I've managed to get in touch with the current headmaster who has promised to meet me at the school after lunch to go through his records. He wasn't there when they would have attended so he does not have any personal recollection of them, but he was very helpful.'

'Good,' replied Carmichael. 'Is the school nearby?'

'Yes,' replied Cooper. 'It's St Mark's Roman Catholic School in Holland Bridge.'

'I have a friend whose younger brother went there,' interrupted Watson. 'If you like I'll ask him if he knew them?'

'Can't do any harm,' replied Cooper.

Officers from Lancashire Police made three arrests that morning in connection with the fraud and race fixing. Charles De Vere was arrested at his house while he was having breakfast and Stan Foster was apprehended at his kennels as he was loading up six of his dogs into the transporter to go to that morning's races at White City. As a direct result of his conversation with Penny before Steve left for work, a third person was detained, Vicky Jenkins, one of Stan Foster's leading kennel girls. The three suspects were all driven independently to Kirkwood police station and placed in separate interview rooms.

At first Charles De Vere protested his total innocence, then, confronted with Lillia Monroe's bank statements that showed payments going into his bank and with photocopies of the English translation of key parts of Lillia's diary, he decided to remain silent.

Stan Foster was very angry at being arrested. From the outset he denied any wrongdoing and, despite being questioned for over three hours, remained steadfast to his story that he had neither been involved in, nor knew of any improper activities involving the greyhounds in his charge.

Carmichael had decided to leave Vicky

Jenkins until last. He had asked the arresting officers to allow Foster to be taken away before she was apprehended and at no time during either of their interrogations were the interviewing officers allowed to mention that Vicky Jenkins had also been arrested. When Carmichael and Rachel Dalton entered the interview room, Vicky had already been sitting there with her duty solicitor for more than two hours.

Carmichael looked at his watch and then turned on the tape recorder. 'It is now twelve-thirteen pm on Tuesday twenty-first August,' he said slowly. 'This interview is commencing with Victoria Jenkins at Kirkwood police station in relation to charges of fraud and race fixing. In attendance is her solicitor Daniel Garner and conducting the interview are Inspector Steve Carmichael and DC Rachel Dalton.'

Vicky Jenkins remained silent but looked very frightened.

'Now, Vicky,' said Carmichael. 'We have reason to believe that for some considerable time a number of people have been engaged in race fixing involving greyhounds trained at Stan Foster's kennels. We understand that you may have been involved in this activity. Can you please explain to us what you know about what has been going on and what your involvement was?'

'I don't know what you are talking about,' she said calmly.

'Are you saying you have no knowledge of any sort of practices undertaken at Stan Foster's kennels that may have led to some of the dogs' performances being affected?' said Dalton.

'Before you answer, Vicky, you need to understand that we know that dogs have been nobbled at Stan Foster's kennels. We also know that large sums of money have been won and lost as a result, and you should also know that, as a result of these activities, up to three people may have been murdered,' said Carmichael firmly. 'I am sure that you were not involved in the murders and I'm also willing to believe that your share of the spoils was fairly minor, but we are sure that you were involved.'

Vicky looked anxiously at her solicitor, who nodded at her as if to prompt her to talk. 'I didn't do anything more than I was told,' she said nervously. 'I just fed some of the dogs like I was told.'

Carmichael was relieved that at least this suspect was not going to deny her involvement. 'What do you mean?' he asked.

Vicky again looked at her legal representative, who again nodded to her to continue. 'Well, normally when we know we are racing a dog we don't feed it that day until after the race. But on some occasions I was told to feed dogs that I knew were running. But that's all I did.'

'Who told you to do this?' asked Rachel.

'I'm not saying,' replied Vicky. 'It's not for me to say.'

'I can understand that you don't want to get anyone into trouble, but you must have realised that what you were doing was slowing down the dogs thus giving the others an unfair advantage,' said Steve.

Vicky shrugged her shoulders.

'Look, Vicky,' said Rachel. 'We know that you were seeing Charles De Vere. You were spotted with him by a witness who says that you were kissing and cuddling. Do you deny that?'

Vicky was now clearly feeling a little uncomfortable. 'We went out a few times, that's all,' she said. 'I know he's married, but he told me that his relationship with her was all over.' As she spoke Vicky started to cry.

Carmichael pushed a box of tissues in Vicky's direction. 'It's none of our business,' he said, 'if you were having a relationship with Charles De Vere. We are not interested in that. What we are interested in is the fact that you were persuaded by him to overfeed his dogs just before races. In so doing you were helping him, Stan Foster and at least one other person to commit fraud. Don't you see that?'

Vicky nodded. 'Yes,' she replied.

'So, can you confirm that it was Charles De Vere and Stan Foster who instructed you to feed the dogs?' Rachel asked.

Vicky shook her head. 'No, it was just Charles,' she replied. 'Stan didn't know anything about it. He would never do anything like that.'

At that moment the interview room door opened and Watson walked in.

'Sorry to interrupt, sir,' he said, 'but I need to talk with you.'

Carmichael looked at his watch. 'Interview suspended at twelve-thirty-five,' he said before turning off the tape recorder. 'Why don't you get Vicky and Mr Garner a coffee, Rachel?' continued Carmichael as he left the room.

When she got word of the arrests of her husband and of Stan Foster, Hannah De Vere drove straight to the station. For more than two hours she had been waiting in reception for an opportunity to speak with Steve. The duty sergeant had told her that she would have to wait until he had finished his interviews. However, when Hannah demanded to and eventually did speak with Chief Inspector Hewitt, he decided that her attendance at the station should be made known to Carmichael and that he should be interrupted and told to speak to her.

When Steve entered the waiting room Hannah De Vere stood up and walked over to him.

'You've made a big mistake here,' she said. 'You've arrested the wrong man.'

'Please sit down, Hannah,' Steve said calmly. 'First of all, nobody has been formally charged, but I'm afraid that all our evidence points to your husband being very much involved with Lillia Monroe in a major fraud.'

'Oh, I know he's guilty as hell,' replied Hannah with little emotion. 'And I am not surprised to hear that Lillia was the brains behind this, but Stan Foster is entirely innocent. Please believe me when I say that Stan would never do anything like this.'

Steve was shocked. He had fully expected Hannah to be there to plead for leniency, but for Charles not Stan Foster. 'I see,' was all he could say.

'I was suspicious of the relationship Charles was developing with Lillia a few months ago,' Hannah confided. 'I had assumed it was just him trying it on with her, and foolishly I thought she had gone along with him. That's why I severed our relationship. I should have known that she was too smart to just want him. It was the money they could make from the race fixing that she was interested in. It was only the other day, when he admitted what he had done, that I realised what had gone on.'

'But how are you so sure that Stan Foster is not involved?' Steve asked.

'Because, Inspector,' she replied, 'Stan and I have been romantically involved for the past twelve months. He is an honest man and I am convinced that he would never get involved in anything as devious as race fixing.'

'I see,' said Carmichael for a second time. 'And does your husband know about your relationship with Stan Foster?'

'Of course not,' replied Hannah. 'He is so busy in his own world of lies and deceit that he probably hasn't the time or wit to see what is under his nose.'

Carmichael remained stunned. 'Can I ask, were you aware of his relationship with one of Stan's kennel girls?'

'So that's how he did it,' replied Hannah. 'I was wondering how he managed to slow down his dogs. Which unlucky girl was it?'

'I am not at liberty to say,' replied Carmichael.

'I knew he was seeing someone as the fool left the receipt for his last nocturnal tryst in his jacket pocket for me to find. It was a night of passion no doubt at the Lindley Hotel, on the evening of Friday the tenth of August.'

As Steve heard this he froze. 'Are you saying that your husband stayed at the Lindley on the tenth of August?'

'Yes,' replied Hannah, not realising the significance of what she was saying. 'I probably still have the receipt at home, I'll bring it in if you want.'

'Thanks. You must excuse me, I have to go,' said Carmichael.

'But what about Stan?' shouted Hannah as he left the room.

Carmichael did not respond.

Carmichael summoned Watson and Rachel to his office.

'There's been a major development,' he

said excitedly. 'It would appear that Charles De Vere met someone at the Lindley on the evening before Lillia was murdered. Given that she used that hotel and given that her body was found very close to the hotel, it could well be that Lillia stayed there that night with Charles De Vere. If that is the case then he is more than just a fraudster.'

'What do you want us to do?' asked Watson.

'First of all I want you to finish the interviews with De Vere and Foster. Take statements from them both and keep them here overnight. Rachel, you take a statement from Vicky. Find out if it was her who was with him that night at the Lindley. But then let her go. She's just a small cog in the machine.'

'What will you be doing, sir?' enquired Rachel.

'I'm going back to the Lindley to check their tapes for that night,' he replied as he headed for the door. 'But call me later and let me know what you get from those three. Also, if Cooper calls in, ask him to call me at home with an update on how he's doing trying to track down Peter Monroe.'

Watson and Dalton remained in Carmichael's office after the boss had left.

'Is all this illicit and secretive sex getting

you going too?' he said, much to Rachel's disdain.

'What are you on about,' replied Rachel angrily.

'Nothing,' replied Watson with an irritating smirk. 'It's just that I couldn't help noticing a little secret petting going on with you and the translator this morning.'

Rachel was horrified. 'I don't know what you are talking about,' she said, although her shaking voice clearly could not hide her guilt.

'So how did it all go?' asked Penny as Steve entered the kitchen, arms laden with tapes. 'Did they both confess?'

Steve nervously shrugged his shoulders. 'It didn't go quite as I'd expected, but I was half right.'

Penny was confused. 'Which half?' she asked.

'The Charles De Vere half mainly,' he replied. 'But your piece of information about Charles and Vicky Jenkins has been a real help, and Hannah De Vere has provided some information that I think could prove to be a major breakthrough.'

Chapter 27

Steve eased himself back into his favourite armchair, pressed the button on the remote control and started to watch the security tapes from the Lindley Hotel for the evening of August 10th. He had met with Sarah Pennington that afternoon and together they had gone through the register for that day. Unfortunately they could not find any record of Lillia Monroe booking in under her own name or that of Mrs Burton, nor of Charles De Vere checking in that evening. Only two couples had booked in that night, Mr and Mrs Reynolds and Mr and Mrs Symonds. Steve was sure that the tapes would reveal that one of these would be De Vere and he hoped that the other would be Lillia Monroe. He was only a few minutes into the first tape when Robbie entered the room.

'Hi, son,' he said. 'How was your day?'

Robbie looked fed up. 'Pretty boring really,' he said as he flopped into the sofa. Steve switched off the tape that he was watching.

'Your mum tells me that you're going to stay on at the supermarket.'

Robbie did not reply.

'I think it's great that you are earning some money,' said Steve. 'And if that's what you want then I just wanted to let you know that that's fine with me.'

Robbie stared at his dad in amazement. 'What? You're OK with me working in Ainsworth's and giving up school!' he said.

'Absolutely,' replied Steve. 'You are old enough to make your own mind up. So it's not for me or your mum to tell you what to do with your life.'

Robbie was confused. He had expected his dad to have the same opinion as his mum. 'Well, I've not fully decided,' he said. 'I guess it depends on my GCSE results.'

'Of course,' Steve responded. 'If they are good then I can understand you wanting to maybe stay on at school, but I suspect that you're expecting the worst. Is that how it is?'

Robbie thought for a moment before replying. 'I should be OK in History and I'm always getting good marks in Geography, so I should be OK with those subjects, but I'm not so sure about the others.'

'Well, I'm sure you did your best,' continued his father. 'And once you get your results I'm sure you'll make the right decision.'

By now Robbie was totally flummoxed. He had never heard his dad talk like this and, although he was pleased that he was not getting a hard time, he found the way the conversation was going difficult to cope with.

'I have to go,' he said as he got up off the sofa and made his way out of the room.

'Is Dad OK?' he whispered to his mother as he passed her in the hallway. 'He's acting really strange.'

As Steve started watching the second of the tapes he received a call from Rachel. 'Hello, sir,' she said. 'Foster is still adamant that he had no involvement in the fraud, De Vere is refusing to say anything or make a statement, but before she was released Vicky Jenkins confirmed that she had stayed that night at the Lindley with De Vere. They booked in under the name of Mr and Mrs Reynolds.'

'I know,' replied Steve despondently as he saw them on TV walking up the drive. When he had finished the call Steve switched off the television and sat back in his chair.

'Are you OK?' asked Penny as she sat down next to him.

'I don't know, dear,' he replied. 'We've had three murders and to be honest I'm no nearer solving the case now than I was ten days ago.'

'Never mind,' said Penny. 'You've solved a serious fraud and you've caught the infamous village burglar, so you've not been idle.'

'Actually,' said Steve with a smile, 'you should have seen the look on Hewitt's face yesterday when I told him that the burglar was a community copper. It was priceless.'

That night Steve could not settle. He tossed and turned, but no matter how hard he tried to get to sleep his thoughts kept returning to the main points from the three murders he was now investigating. He was still convinced that Lillia's diary held the key to the identity of the perpetrator of the crimes, however, the realisation that he was no nearer finding the killer than he had been when Lillia's body had been found made him very anxious. It was almost 2 am before he finally went to sleep, by which time he had persuaded himself that the team's most immediate task was to find Bradley Monroe's brother. He also accepted that he had no evidence to link Stan Foster with the betting scam that De Vere and Lillia had been running. His last thought before he went to sleep was that he would release Stan Foster the following morning.

'Let me get this straight,' said Hewitt. 'Lillia Monroe was known to have had an affair with the latest victim, with whom she was involved in a fraud against her company. She was presently having an affair with the Managing Director at Gemini Technologies, who may or may not have been involved in the fiddle.'

'Correct,' replied Carmichael, 'but we think this was probably only an affair'.

'Also, Lillia was involved in a greyhound betting fraud with Charles De Vere, who was the husband of her friend and who is known to have stayed with a young lady at the Lindley Hotel on the night before Lillia was killed, which is the hotel used by Lillia and her boss for their weekly assignations and coincidentally is only a few miles from where Lillia was killed the following morning, by someone who you feel she knew well.'

Steve was impressed by his boss's succinct summary of the facts. 'Yes, sir,' he said. 'That's about it.'

'She sounds like a right one,' said Hewitt. 'Certainly she appears to have had few scruples,' agreed Carmichael.

Hewitt leant back in his chair and looked up at the ceiling. 'Just run the betting fraud past me again?' he asked.

'Well,' said Carmichael. 'It works like this. De Vere and his accomplice would try and slow down some of his dogs on the day they were due to race. We think this was done purely by giving them a good feed. I understand that the normal practice is for dogs not to be fed on the day they run.'

'So in doing this they were actually trying to stop their own dogs from winning?' confirmed Hewitt.

'That's correct,' replied Carmichael.

'But if they don't win how do they profit?' asked Hewitt, who was clearly not that familiar with current gambling practices.

'In recent times it's become really commonplace for people to bet online,' said Carmichael. 'What De Vere would do is tell his girlfriend, who was a kennel maid at the kennels, to feed certain dogs. He would then advise Lillia somehow which dogs were being fed. She would then offer good odds to people online and in effect bet against these dogs winning. Seeing good odds being offered, people would then bet on these dogs with Lillia to win and of course because the dogs had been fed, they would be slower and thus more than likely lose.'

'I see,' replied Hewitt. 'So in effect Lillia was defrauding those who were accepting the bets, based upon her knowledge that the dogs in question had been unnecessarily fed.'

'Correct,' replied Carmichael.

'Actually,' commented Hewitt, with a certain degree of approval, 'that's quite clever.'

'But also quite illegal,' replied Carmichael.

'Exactly,' replied Hewitt. 'So what is your plan of action now, Inspector?'

'We intend to charge De Vere with fraud,' said Carmichael. 'We will also question him and Vicky Jenkins on their movements on the morning of Saturday the eleventh of August, which is when we know Lillia was killed. To be honest I'm not sure that De Vere knew either Bradley Monroe or Tom Sharwood so he may not be our man but, as you say, he was involved with Lillia in the betting scam and was near to where she died, so we have to look at him as a potential suspect.'

Hewitt nodded his approval. 'So, who else do you have as suspects?'

Steve shuffled uneasily in his chair. 'Well, to be honest, we have a few possibilities, but nobody that we feel strongly is our killer.'

'Who are the most likely suspects?' probed Hewitt.

'The people we are currently investigating are Ralf Marsh, who was Lillia's boss and the person who was having the affair with her. Then there's the company secretary, a lady called Ruth Andrews, who we know did not get on at all with Lillia, and we are also trying to locate Peter Monroe who is Bradley Monroe's brother and who Lillia writes fondly of in her diary.'

'And where does Peter Monroe live?' asked Hewitt.

'At the moment we don't have an address for him,' replied Carmichael. 'However, Cooper is on to this and I'm hoping we will get a breakthrough there soon.'

'And that's it, is it?' said Hewitt despondently.

'We have a few other people who we need to talk to some more,' replied Carmichael. 'The problem is that it's proving very hard to find a connection between the three murders. It's equally hard to find people who knew all three.'

'Then maybe you should be thinking more about there being more than one murderer,' said Hewitt.

'Maybe,' replied Carmichael. 'However, my instinct tells me that the murders were all committed by the same person. I'm also pretty sure that the answer to this riddle is in Lillia's diary. I'm going to spend some more time today re-reading it in case we missed something the first time.'

'I'll leave this to your good judgment, Inspector,' replied Hewitt, 'but please heed my advice and do not close off any avenues at this stage. It would be highly embarrassing for all of us if we did that and it was later proved to have been a mistake.'

'I agree,' replied Carmichael. 'We'll certainly explore all possible lines of enquiry until things become clearer.'

Carmichael left the morning briefing with Hewitt feeling rather low. As he walked down the corridor towards the main incident room, he reflected on the lack of progress he and the team were making and couldn't help worrying that there may be more murders yet, before the killer was apprehended.

In comparison to that of her husband, Wednesday morning had fared much better for Penny. Not only had she had the unusual pleasure of seeing her eldest daughter up and dressed before 10 am, she had also been informed by Robbie over breakfast that he had changed his mind about staying on at the supermarket and that he had now decided to go back to school that September to start his A Level courses after all. In addition, just as she was leaving the house to take Natalie to the stables and much to her surprise, she received a call from the appliance firm to inform her that an engineer would be round that afternoon to mend her cooker.

'That's excellent news,' said Penny as she replaced the handset. 'It looks like you may get a proper meal tonight everyone.'

Jemma and Robbie just ignored their mother and although Natalie smiled, she was not bothered in the slightest at this news. She had quite enjoyed the various microwaved and takeaway meals that she had been having during the last week, so a return to her mother's cooking was not such great news as far as she was concerned.

When Penny arrived at the stables, Hannah came across to talk with to her. 'Morning, Natalie,' she said with no hint of a smile. 'Why don't you take out Lucy this morning for a good long ride?' Normally Natalie had to spend the first two hours at the stables mucking out before she could ride Lucy, so on hearing this news she quickly jumped out of the car and ran towards the stables.

'Penny,' said Hannah sheepishly. 'Did Steve mention anything to you about Charles and Stan?'

'He did say that they were both at the station,' replied Penny trying hard not to say too much.

'Did he mention that I went over to see him yesterday?' asked Hannah.

'Well, briefly.' Penny said, although Steve had told her everything that had happened.

'This may seem strange to you, Penny,' said Hannah, 'but I have no interest in what happens to Charles. As far as I'm concerned he has only himself to blame. But Stan is totally blameless in all this.'

'Look, Hannah,' said Penny firmly. 'Steve has not shared that much of the details with me, he can't. However, I'm sure that if Stan Foster is innocent then he has nothing to worry about.'

Chapter 28

'Great news, sir,' exclaimed Cooper as Steve entered the incident room. 'I didn't get too much from my visit to see the headmaster of St Mark's yesterday, but Marc's friend's brother has come up trumps. We've managed to get a work address and mobile number for Peter Monroe.'

'That's fantastic news,' Carmichael said, his voice full of excitement. 'Where does he live?'

'He's not that far,' replied Cooper. 'He works at a wildlife park close to Liverpool. We've tried to reach him on his mobile but he's not answering. Rachel has called his work but they said that he was not there. He was on leave and was due back yesterday, but he never turned up. However, they have given us his home address, so Rachel and I are planning to drive over to see if we can locate him.'

'OK, you two get over there now,' ordered Carmichael, 'but make sure you alert the local force so they know what you are doing.'

Cooper smiled and left the room, followed closely by Rachel Dalton.

'What shall we do while they are doing that?' asked Watson.

'I want to interview Foster and De Vere again,' replied Carmichael. 'Then I'm going to spend a few more hours reading Lillia's diary.'

Stan Foster's youthful looks did not reveal his real age. Although he had recently turned forty, he would have easily passed for a man ten years younger. Normally Stan was an amiable, patient man, however, having spent twenty-four hours in police custody, his usual poise had long deserted him by the time Carmichael and Watson entered the interview room.

'Good morning,' Carmichael said as he sat down across the table. 'There are a few more questions we need to ask you.'

Foster folded his arms and took a deep breath. 'I've told your colleagues all I know,' he said, the stress and frustration clearly noticeable in his voice. 'I have had no involvement at all in any race fixing. I would be an idiot to do that and I may be many things but I'm not a fool.'

Carmichael watched Foster's body language as he spoke and he now had no doubt that Foster was innocent. 'We are not going to take this any further with you, Mr Foster,' he said calmly. 'I realise that you have been here for some time, but I'm sure you can understand that we are just doing our job, and that you needed to be questioned given that the alleged race fixing occurred with dogs in your charge at your kennels.'

For the first time in twenty-four hours, Stan Foster was able to relax. 'Are you saying that I'm to be released and will not be charged?'

'Yes, you are free to go,' replied Carmichael. 'However, we would like you to help us, as we have a few more questions we need answers to.'

A now very relieved Foster nodded his agreement.

'Firstly,' said Carmichael, 'can you tell me how many dogs you train for Charles De Vere?'

'He is one of my major owners,' replied Foster. 'He has six dogs with me at present.'

'Did you have no idea at all what was going on?' Carmichael asked.

Foster shook his head. 'Absolutely none,' he replied. 'His dogs had been on a bit of a bad run of late, but I had no inkling of anything underhand going on at the kennels.'

'When you say bad run, what do you mean?' asked Watson.

'Well,' replied Foster, 'Charles's dogs are all well bred. He only ever buys dogs with good pedigrees. Of course, that is no guarantee that they will be successful, but it helps your chances.'

'And were his doing worse than you would expect?' asked Carmichael.

'Up to about four or five months ago they were doing fine,' said Foster. 'On average I'd say he would get a winner in every two or three runs. However, lately this had gone down to about a winner only every five or six races, so a noticeable decline.'

'What did you think was happening?' Carmichael asked.

'I didn't know,' said Foster. 'I had the vets to them on a few occasions but they were always passed as fit, so I just thought he was having an unlucky run.'

'What about Vicky Jenkins?' interjected Watson. 'Did you suspect her at all?'

Foster smiled. 'I had an idea that she and Charles were having some sort of relationship. He was always coming on to her and although at first I don't think she was interested, of late she seemed to enjoy his interest in her and would also do her fair bit of flirting with him. Having said that, I had no reason not to trust Vicky and I would never have expected her to get involved in anything like this.'

'OK,' replied Carmichael. 'We've taken enough of your time so you can go.'

Stan Foster got up from his chair and to Steve's surprise, held out his hand. 'Thank you for believing in me,' he said. Steve shook his hand and escorted him and his solicitor out of the interview room.

'Out of interest,' said Carmichael. 'How much does a greyhound cost to buy and to keep in training?'

Stan Foster shrugged his shoulders. 'That depends very much on the pedigree of the dog. But a goodish dog will set you back about five thousand to buy at eighteen months of age and will cost you about two-fifty a month to keep at my kennels.'

'Not cheap then,' replied Carmichael.

'That all depends on how well they do and what you call expensive,' said Foster. 'Charles must have spent about fifty thousand on his six dogs and he gets a bit of a discount as he has so many. I think we charge him a thousand a month, well, I should say we did. After all this I'm going to tell him to find another trainer.'

'What about Vicky Jenkins?' Steve asked.

'She will be sacked as soon as I get back to the kennels,' replied Foster.

After Stan Foster had left the station Carmichael and Watson entered interview room two, where Charles De Vere and his solicitor were silently waiting. Carmichael turned on the recorder.

'Interview with Charles De Vere and his solicitor Julian Alcock commencing at 11:45 am on Wednesday 22nd August, investigating officers are Inspector Steve Carmichael and Sergeant Marc Watson. Mr De Vere,' said Carmichael. 'You have been held here at Kirkwood station for over twenty-four hours and have refused to answer any of our questions in connection with our investigation into fraud involving your greyhounds at Stan Foster's kennels.'

De Vere and his counsel remained quiet and motionless.

'I want to give you this last opportunity to put your side of the story before you are formally charged. Are you willing to cooperate?'

De Vere remained impassive and silent.

'Fair enough,' said Carmichael. 'Let me just share with you and your counsel what evidence we have about the fraud and your association with this crime'. Steve paused for a moment before continuing.

'In the course of our investigations into the murder of Lillia Monroe, we have read her diary. In that she clearly implicates you as her associate in fixing the races of some of your greyhounds, which you kennel with Stan Foster. We are satisfied that Stan Foster has had no part in this swindle, however, it's clear from regular bank transfers from Lillia Monroe to you that she was paying you five hundred pounds every two weeks. This is interesting as it appears to be exactly the sum of money you pay Stan Foster each month for kennel fees. We know that Lillia regularly bet online against your dogs winning, and had almost a hundred per cent success rate, even though your dogs are all well bred and with excellent pedigrees. Also we have a statement from Vicky Jenkins that you and she were having a relationship, we have CCTV taped evidence that you and she spent the evening of the tenth of August at the Lindley Hotel, and Vicky has also confessed that she regularly fed some of your dogs that were due to race that day upon your direct instructions, and contrary to common practice.'

De Vere remained totally expressionless.

'Are you still going to maintain silence about all this?' asked Watson, who was clearly annoyed by De Vere's lack of cooperation.

'No comment,' replied De Vere arrogantly.

Carmichael smiled. 'In that case we are now going to formally charge you with fraud. You will remain in custody until we are able to put you in front of a magistrate.'

De Vere continued to adopt his deadpan demeanour.

'Before we do so, however, I'd like to ask you some questions about an even more serious crime, namely the murders of Lillia and Bradley Monroe and the murder of Tom Sharwood,' said Carmichael.

'This is ridiculous,' replied De Vere's solicitor. 'Surely you are not suggesting that my client is a murderer, Inspector?'

'Well, he was involved with Lillia in a fraud and, as I said before, he is known to have been leaving the Lindley Hotel on the morning that Lillia was murdered. The Lindley Hotel is just a few miles away from the place where she was killed. So I think it's reasonable for us to investigate this link.'

For the first time De Vere looked ruffled.

'The allegations about the fraud are total rubbish,' he said. 'So much so that I'm not going to even waste my time with you on that particular issue. However I will help you with anything you need to know about Lillia's murder. I have no issue with that and will agree to write a full statement about my activities on the evening of the tenth of August and the morning of eleventh August, if that will help.'

This surprised Carmichael. 'Excellent,' he said. 'That will be very helpful. Excuse us for a moment.' Carmichael and Watson left the interview room.

'Do you think De Vere might be our murderer?' asked Watson.

'I doubt it,' replied Carmichael. 'I just don't see it. Also it's unlikely that he knew Bradley well, if at all, and I certainly don't think he would have known Sharwood, so unless we have more than one murderer, I'm pretty sure De Vere is not our man.'

'Maybe there is more than one killer?' suggested Watson.

'That's what Hewitt thinks too,' said Carmichael. 'But I'm pretty sure we are looking for just one murderer.'

Watson shrugged his shoulders. 'So what do we do now?' he said.

'Well, Marc, you stay here and take De Vere's statement then formally charge him with fraud,' said Carmichael. 'I'm going to get some lunch and then get back to Lillia's diary.'

Chapter 29

It was after 5:30 pm when Steve left the station, aggravated that he had learned nothing new from the diary and a little perturbed that neither Cooper nor Rachel Dalton had called him with an update on their attempts to track down Peter Monroe.

By the time Steve arrived home that evening he was totally exhausted. The very last thing he wanted to do that night was to take part in Robbie Robertson's Wednesday evening pub quiz at the Railway Tavern. However, his wife had other ideas and Penny could be very persuasive when she wanted. Being tired and seeing that she was so keen to go, Steve could not muster the energy to protest for too long and inevitably he eventually capitulated to her persistent demands. 'OK, you win,' he said at last. 'I'll have a quick shower and then we'll go.'

He had spent most of the afternoon in his office reading Lillia's diary over and over again. Although he now knew for sure that she was not an escort but a very accomplished manipulator and a fraudster, and although he had now put names to the various pseudonyms and initials she had used, Steve still felt that the notes she had written had yet more to reveal. He was sure that something in her writings would expose her killer but was frustrated that, despite reading her words time and time again, he could not find what he was searching for.

Penny was mightily relieved that Steve had released Stan Foster, not just because his temporary incarceration had clearly been of major concern to Hannah, but also she had been worried that, should Stan have remained in custody, this would have put a major dampener on her plans for their anniversary surprise. Her cooker now fixed, Penny had prepared the family a large cottage pie, so she was pleased when Steve arrived home at a reasonable time. She was not overly keen to go to the pub quiz, however she wanted to make sure Steve had at least a few hours where he could take his mind off the case, and she knew that a few pints should guarantee that he would not spend that evening in his study reading through Lillia Monroe's diary. As usual she was right and, despite his protestations, as soon as Steve had consumed his first pint he appeared to have temporarily forgotten about the case.

At 8:30 the quiz began. Penny and Steve joined Sam Crouch and Bartholomew Green to form a team they called The Hell-raisers. Round one was a sports round which went well. Steve had a good knowledge of football and rugby and was able to answer most of the questions on these sports, however he was pleased that Bartholomew was on the team to answer the three cricket questions in that round. Round two was on spelling, which brought Penny into her own. At the end of that round The Hell-raisers were in joint first place with 17 points out of a possible 20.

'We're looking good,' said Bartholomew. 'By the way, Steve, your mobile is flashing.'

Steve took his phone from his breast pocket and looked at the name on the screen. 'Sorry, Pen,' he said. 'I'll have to take this, it's Cooper.' He did not see his wife's look of disdain as he made his way out of the bar and took the call.

'Hello, sir,' said Cooper. 'Sorry it's taken so long to call, we've had an interesting afternoon.'

'Did you find Peter Monroe?' he asked.

'No,' replied Cooper. 'He's not turned up yet either at work or at his house. The local police have been very helpful though. They have obtained a court order to allow us to break into his house. We are there now and they are just about to make an entrance.'

'I see,' said Carmichael. 'Let me know what you find when you are in there.'

'Will do, sir,' replied Cooper.

When Steve returned to the table round three had ended and The Hell-raisers were now trailing after only scoring 4 out of 10 on history.

'We could have done with you in that round,' said Penny. 'We struggled badly.'

'Sorry, team. I'll try not to get distracted again,' said Steve. 'Let me get everyone some more drinks.'

'I'm OK,' said Penny, who still had half her drink left.

'Me too,' said Sam.

'How about you, Barney?' Steve asked. 'What will you have?'

'I'll have a pint of bitter please, Steve,'

came back the reply, 'and it's Bartholomew, Barney's the ugly brother.'

Steve smiled, made his apology and walked over to the bar to order the drinks. As he waited for Katie to bring over his drinks, Steve's mind wandered to what Bartholomew had just said. His thoughts then meandered to one of the first statements that he had read from Lillia's diary. At the time he had not fully appreciated what she meant, but he did now.

'Katie, can you take the drinks over to my table? Here's a ten pound note, keep the change.'

Penny watched with amazement as her husband rushed out of the pub clutching his phone. 'He didn't take long to break that promise, did he?' she said to Sam.

Chapter 30

At 10:27 am the following morning Carmichael's car pulled into the car park outside the pathology lab. In keeping with his obsession with time, Carmichael had calculated the night before that the 18 mile journey, which was mainly along quiet country lanes should take him between 30 and 35 minutes. Having negotiated the trip in just 32 minutes, Steve was pretty pleased with himself, especially given the fact that at no time had he exceeded the speed limit to attain his target. He shoved the gear lever into neutral, turned off the ignition and strode confidently into the lab.

As instructed, Cooper, Watson and Rachel Dalton were already in Dr Stock's small office when he arrived.

'I understand that you have cracked the case,' remarked Stock.

Carmichael acknowledged Stock's comments with a knowing smile.

'Do you all have with you the items I asked you to bring?' he said.

The three police officers glanced at each other.

'Well, actually,' said Watson, 'I looked high and low and I could not find the bag anywhere.'

'What bag are you talking about?' asked Stock.

'The bag that Bradley Monroe left at the house when PC Tyler kindly allowed him to drop in on the way here,' replied Carmichael. 'I called Marc last night and asked him to go back to Monroe's house and bring the bag that Monroe left that day back here.'

'So where is it?' asked Watson.

'It's here,' said Cooper, who held up the case they had seen in Monroe's house the week before.

'It's even still got the Lufthansa tag on the handle,' said Watson. 'So where did you find it?'

'At Peter Monroe's house,' replied Cooper.

'Yes, after I called you, Marc, I spoke with Cooper and asked him to go back to Peter Monroe's flat and see if he could find it there. I was pretty sure he would,' said Carmichael.

'I'm confused,' said Watson. 'How come it got there?'

'Because,' replied Carmichael. 'That's where it should have been, as it belongs to Peter Monroe.'

Watson was no clearer, but decided to wait to hear what else his boss was going to say.

'Did you manage to get what I asked you to bring?' Carmichael asked Rachel.

'Yes,' she said as she held up the A4 envelope she had in her hand. 'It was as you suspected: Peter and Bradley were twins. I have copies of their birth certificates here.'

Carmichael smiled broadly. 'I thought as

much,' he said with glee.

'I'm curious how you managed to come to that conclusion,' Rachel said.

'It was a bit of luck really,' replied Carmichael. 'I had been wondering about something that Lillia had written in her diary. It was one of the initial things I spotted when I first started reading it and was there for all to see in plain English.'

'What was that?' asked Watson.

'It was this line,' said Carmichael, who opened the diary to the page he had marked.

'I sometimes think that PM would have been a better choice than Brad, but he's not so good-looking ... ha ha!!!'

'I don't see how that leads you to believe that they were twins?' said Watson.

'Well,' replied Carmichael. 'It just seemed a strange thing to put down. If she had missed off the *ha ha* part then maybe you would just assume that what she was saying was her honest opinion. However, putting *ha ha* suggests she is joking, which means that either Peter was better looking than Bradley in her eyes, which was my initial assumption, or that they looked the same. I'm not suggesting I am an expert on how women would rate men's looks, but I think most would have said that Bradley was a good-looking man. If that is the case then the only logical assumption would be that they looked the same.'

Rachel nodded her head. 'Yes, that makes sense.'

'It had been nagging me for ages, but what she meant only dawned on me last night when coincidentally I made the mistake of calling someone who I know to be a twin the wrong Christian name. When he corrected me it suddenly came to me that Peter and Bradley were twins too.'

There was a moment's silence as Watson, Cooper, Rachel and Dr Stock all considered the implications of what had just been revealed.

'So was it Peter Monroe or Bradley Monroe who killed Lillia?' asked Watson.

Carmichael smiled again. 'I think I know the answer to that too, but first I need to know if you managed to get the other items I asked you to collect?'

Watson and Cooper simultaneously each held up a pair of shoes.

'I'm now completely lost,' said Dr Stock.

Carmichael enjoyed the thrill of seeing such a clearly intelligent pathologist struggling to make sense of what he was hearing.

'OK,' said Carmichael proudly. 'Let me share with you all what I think happened.' His small audience waited in silence as Carmichael began to enlighten them.

'I suspect that Bradley Monroe became concerned about his wife's activities. Maybe he found her diary or maybe he just wondered about her sudden wealth. He may even have been suspicious of her relationship with Ralf Marsh. Whatever led to his apprehension, I believe that he colluded with his brother to do some investigations or maybe even to have her murdered. They carefully chose that weekend as it was a perfect opportunity for Bradley to create for himself the ideal alibi of being on business in Germany.'

'So was the murderer Peter or Bradley?' asked Watson.

'And also,' interjected Dr Stock, 'is it Peter or Bradley lying there in the other room?'

'I am not one hundred per cent sure, but I suspect that the person PC Tyler collected from the airport and drove to Bradley Monroe's house that morning was Peter Monroe,' said Carmichael. 'The fact that the suitcase he had with him was found in Peter's house suggests to me that the twins did the switch at Bradley's house while PC Tyler waited downstairs.'

'So Bradley was already in the house when Peter arrived?' asked Rachel.

'Yes,' replied Carmichael. 'I think it was Peter Monroe who arrived and went upstairs, but they quickly changed clothes and it was Bradley who came down and left the house with PC Tyler.'

'That's amazing,' said Cooper. 'But surely, if that was true, the people Peter Monroe met in Germany would recognise that he was not Bradley?'

'Why would they?' proclaimed Carmichael. 'If you recall, when we were checking out Bradley's alibi, we found out that he had not met his colleagues in Germany before so why would they suspect? Also, he was mainly at the hotel or at an exhibition, so he would not even need to try and fake any specific work-related knowledge. No, I think this switch was carefully chosen by Bradley. It gave him the opportunity to be in two places at one time.'

'But Peter must then have been in on the deception and presumably on the murder too?' said Watson.

'I'm not sure about that,' replied Carmichael. 'He would obviously have been in on the deception, but I'm not sure about the murder.'

'And the dead body in my lab?' said Dr Stock. 'Are you saying it's Peter or Bradley?'

'If I'm correct,' responded Carmichael, 'that should be quite easy to establish.'

'How?' asked Rachel.

Carmichael again smiled widely; he was clearly enjoying revealing his thoughts. 'That is where the shoes come in,' he said. 'When PC Tyler left the house with Bradley, he said that Bradley was dressed the same except for his shoes, which he had changed. My guess is that when they did the quick change upstairs they were able to swap clothes easily as they were a similar size, but they had to use different shoes as their feet were not the same size.'

In unison Cooper and Watson checked the shoes they were holding. 'Mine are size nine,' said Cooper, who was holding a pair of Peter's shoes.

'Bradley's are size eleven,' said Watson.

'So all we have to do is to check the shoe size of the body in the lab,' said Carmichael. 'If it is size eleven it's Bradley, but I suspect they will be size nine, which means the person in there is Peter and not Bradley as we had assumed.'

Carmichael, Cooper, Watson and Rachel followed Dr Stock into the adjoining room, where the cold stiff body was laid out on the trolley. Dr Stock partially lifted the sheet to reveal the feet of the corpse. He took the left shoe from Watson and placed it over the left foot of the body. The shoe fitted easily and with a great deal of room around it. He then took the right shoe that Cooper was holding and put it on the right foot of the deceased. As Carmichael had predicted, it was a perfect fit.

Chapter 31

'We need to move quickly,' said Carmichael to his team as they gathered back in Dr Stock's office. 'Marc, I want you to get back to the station and make sure a full description of Bradley Monroe is issued to all police forces, and this gets as much exposure in the press as we can. See if we can get the local TV and radio to make some announcements today. I'm sure Chief Inspector Hewitt will be only too willing to help you in that area.'

'Right you are, sir,' replied Watson as he headed for the exit.

'Cooper and Dalton, we are going to Ralf

Marsh's house. If I'm correct that's where Bradley Monroe is likely to turn up next.'

Bradley Monroe had loved his wife dearly. He knew she was ambitious and he had accepted that she had a tendency to use her looks to her advantage. His suspicions, however, had not been raised until he had found her diary three weeks earlier. Although he could not understand the entries she had written in Estonian, he could work out enough from what he could read to suggest that she was having an affair. She denied this of course, but Bradley was not convinced by her protestations of innocence. He had persuaded Peter to provide him with the alibi he needed so that he could follow his wife and find out for himself what she was up to. He had waited outside Gemini on the Friday. When she left alone and returned to their house that evening he had initially hidden outside the house waiting to see if anyone would come in. Once it had got to 1 am with no sign of her leaving or anyone arriving, Bradley had quietly let himself in and con cealed himself in their spare room. Lil suspected nothing and had no idea that husband was in the house when she mad call to Tom Sharwood at 9:30 on the S

day morning.

Of course Bradley had no idea who his wife was talking to, but, by the way she was speaking, he decided there and then that it was a lover. Being tired from almost no sleep and wracked with jealousy Bradley confronted his wife as soon as she had ended the call. Lillia's pleas of innocence fell on deaf ears and at knifepoint, Bradley made his wife drive them both to the secluded spot by the lake where they had often had romantic walks when they were first married. Here he finally forced a confession from Lillia who by then was very worried as to her fate and saw a full admission as her only possible salvation.

Once she had confessed Lillia noticed her husband become calmer. He put down the knife and she felt safe enough to be able to turn her back on him and walk slowly away down the path to the water's edge. Of course she was wrong in this assumption. As soon as her back was turned Bradley, in a fit of rage, struck her hard from behind with the nearest heavy object he could find. It had taken just one blow for Bradley Monroe to render poor Lillia unconscious and send her limp body into the fast-flowing water at Hardy's weir.

Bradley had been surprised to see his twin brother turn up at his house that Thursday evening. Their agreement was that Peter would go back home and resume his life after they had done the switch. However, the plan had never been to kill Lillia, so when Peter learned the news he was concerned about how this would implicate him. Peter had returned that night to try and persuade Bradley to turn himself in. They had talked well into the early hours of Friday morning, but when it was clear that Bradley was not prepared to agree to his wishes, Peter announced that he was going to tell the police. On hearing this Bradley again became angry. It was then that Peter Monroe's life was also extinguished.

Bradley had never planned to kill either his wife or his brother. But it did not take him long to realise that the police would assume that the dead body they would find in his house was him rather than Peter. He decided that this misunderstanding would give him an ideal opportunity to take his revenge on the two people with whom Lillia had confessed to having had affairs: Tom Sharwood and Ralf Marsh.

With Sharwood now dead, Bradley had just one last task to perform before he could disappear for good, that was the murder of Lillia's latest lover and the person she had confessed to being madly in love with.

When Carmichael, Cooper and Dalton arrived at Marsh's house all looked serene. The Marsh children were merrily playing in the garden and music from the radio was gently emanating through the kitchen window. As the three officers walked up to the door they heard the radio announcer interrupt the music with an urgent message regarding Bradley Monroe. They paused for a moment as they listened to the description that was being read out and the advice that should anyone know of Bradley Monroe's whereabouts, they should not approach him but contact the police straight away.

Allison Marsh had not seen the officers' car arrive, but she had heard the description, which exactly matched the young salesman she had taken through to meet her husband only fifteen minutes earlier.

Carmichael rang the bell three times before he instructed Cooper to go around the back. It was as he rang the bell for a fourth time that the door swung open and the distraught figure of Allison Marsh greeted him and Rachel.

'Come quick, he's been attacked!' she shrieked anxiously. 'Call an ambulance.'

Carmichael and Dalton entered the hall at the same time as Cooper arrived through the kitchen.

'What's going on?' Cooper asked.

'It's my husband,' said Allison who was clearly distressed. 'He's been badly hurt.'

'Phone through for an ambulance, Rachel,' Carmichael shouted. Then grabbing hold of Mrs Marsh by her shoulders, he asked, 'Where is he?'

Allison Marsh led Carmichael and Cooper into her husband's study where they were confronted with not one, but two lifeless figures lying on the floor. One was Ralf Marsh, who looked to the world to be dead, and the second was that of Bradley Monroe. Although he had blood pouring from a cut on his head he was clearly still breathing. Beside Monroe lay the same wooden tray that Steve had seen Mrs Marsh use so expertly to strike her husband on his previous visit. She had clearly replicated her party trick in an attempt to stop Bradley Monroe as he attacked her husband.

The paramedics arrived at the house within

a matter of minutes and transported Ralf Marsh to Kirkwood Hospital. Although still alive, it was obvious that his injuries were serious and the medics had told Rachel they thought his chances of survival were less than fifty per cent.

Bradley Monroe's condition was far less serious. Unlike the man he had just attacked, he regained consciousness fairly quickly and although he too needed to be taken to hospital, it was clear that he would make a quick and full recovery. Paul Cooper was immediately despatched to hospital, handcuffed to a groggy but stable prisoner.

'Once he's been discharged,' Carmichael said, 'I want him to be brought back to the station and booked in. I'll interview him personally this afternoon.'

Cooper nodded as he helped his dazed prisoner clamber into the back of the ambulance.

Carmichael instructed Rachel Dalton to stay at the house with the Marsh girls until they could be collected by a family friend. Her orders were then to join Allison Marsh at the hospital. 'Once you get to the hospital call me,' he said to her. 'I want to know how things with Marsh develop.'

Chapter 32

Compared to the theatrics of his elder sister in the weeks leading up to her A level exam results being released, Robbie Carmichael had made very little fuss about the prospect of receiving his GCSE results. His apparent calm and indifference were merely an impressive façade. Inwardly Robbie was every bit as anxious about his results as his sister had been. Penny had realised this, and as the day got nearer she too had become very apprehensive. Now the day had arrived Robbie was very nervous. He was convinced that his results were going to be bad and the prospect of him having to tell his father was something he did not relish.

For once Penny was relieved when Steve told her that he would be making an early start on that particular Thursday morning. 'Make sure you either telephone or text Robbie to find out how he's done,' she reminded him as he left for work.

As soon as Steve realised that he would not be able to interview Monroe until he had been released from hospital, which he figured would be at the earliest that afternoon, he decided to go one better and call in at home to find out how his son had fared first hand. Steve walked through his front door only a few moments after Robbie had arrived back from school. He could hear Penny's voice in the kitchen, but could not work out what she was saying or even if she was happy or simply trying to lift their son's spirits.

'So, how did you do?' Steve asked as he burst into the kitchen.

Robbie was startled by the unexpected arrival of his dad, but without speaking handed over the sheet of paper that contained his GCSE results.

Steve studied the paper for a moment.

'Well done, son,' he said with a proud smile. 'With results like these you would be wasted just stacking shelves for the rest of your life.'

Bradley Monroe was released from the hospital just after lunchtime, and Cooper had him back at Kirkwood police station and in interview room one before 1 pm. Approximately ten minutes later Carmichael entered the room.

'How did you know it was me?' said the

heavily bandaged detainee.

'It was largely through reading Lillia's diary,' replied Carmichael. Monroe nodded gently as if to suggest he already knew that the diary had been his downfall.

'I should have destroyed that bloody diary,' he said through gritted teeth. 'If I had done that I would have been able to get away and start a new life somewhere else.'

For the next few minutes Bradley Monroe, without any attempt to conceal the truth and with hardly the need to be prompted, gave Carmichael and Cooper a full account of how he had suspected his wife of being unfaithful, how he had persuaded his brother to go to Germany in his place and how he had confronted Lillia and taken her down to the lakeside.

'I wanted to forgive her,' he said, 'but when she said that she loved Marsh I just snapped and the next thing I knew I had hit her hard and she was falling into the water.'

'What about your brother?' Cooper asked. 'How did you come to kill him?'

Monroe fixed his gaze on the table and started to fiddle with the plastic coffee cup in front of him. 'We agreed that he should stay away, but that night he came over to my house late and demanded that we talk. The plan was never for me to kill Lillia, so he was frightened and angry. He told me I had to give myself up and when I refused, he said that he was going to the police to confess to his part and turn me in.'

'So you killed him too?' said Carmichael.

Monroe did not reply but gave a slight nod of his head to show his agreement.

'For the tape, Bradley, can you confirm that you murdered your brother?' Carmichael asked.

'Yes,' replied Monroe, now in tears. 'I killed him.'

'So what about Sharwood and Marsh?' Carmichael asked. 'When did you decide to kill them?'

Monroe wiped his eyes and, for the first time since the interview had started, looked up and stared straight at Carmichael. 'I only decided to kill them once Peter was dead. I sat at home that night wondering what to do. Then it came to me. I figured that you would think he was me, just like your officer did the day we did the switch at my house. I guessed it would give me a perfect alibi, and even if it didn't it would buy me some time before you twigged that the body was Peter's and not mine. So that evening I planned to use those precious few days to get my revenge on

Marsh and Sharwood. I wanted to kill Marsh first, because her relationship with him was the one that had made me kill her, but he was never on his own. So I decided to see to Sharwood and then come back for Marsh later.'

'You took a bit of a risk getting Mrs Marsh to let you into the house, didn't you?' commented Carmichael.

Monroe nodded. 'Yes,' he said. 'I did think of just taking Peter's passport and getting away, but I could not allow Marsh to get away with destroying my marriage and taking her from me. I decided last night that I'd rather see him dead than get away and know that he was still alive. So I decided to just go and do it.'

'You must have realised that you would be identified by Mrs Marsh, or was the plan to kill her too?' asked Carmichael.

Monroe shook his head. 'No, once I'd killed Marsh that was it. I had not made any plans beyond that and may have even given myself up like Peter had asked me to. I wouldn't have hurt his wife though. Let's face it, she was betrayed just as I had been, so why would I want to hurt her?'

Carmichael was sure what Monroe was telling him was the truth. He could see no reason why Monroe would have killed Allison Marsh and as he didn't feel he needed anything more from Monroe at that juncture, decided to turn off the tape.

'Sergeant Cooper will take your statement now, and you will be charged with the murders of your wife, your brother and Tom Sharwood,' said Carmichael.

'What about Marsh?' said Monroe in desperation. 'You're not telling me he is still alive are you?'

'At this moment he's still alive,' Carmichael confirmed, 'but that may not be the case for too much longer.'

Monroe's face reddened and the anger that Carmichael and Cooper saw swelling up inside him was so sudden that it took them by surprise. 'Let's hope he doesn't pull through,' Monroe snarled. 'God knows he deserves to die. I hope he does and I pray it's slowly and if it's in great pain then that's even better.'

Chapter 33

'What is the latest on Ralf Marsh?' Hewitt asked from behind his large wooden desk.

'It's not looking good,' replied Carmichael. 'Rachel Dalton is still there with him and his wife, but she called in about half an hour ago and I'm afraid the outlook is bleak.'

Hewitt sighed. 'Do they not expect him to pull through?' he asked.

'Well, they think he may, but they are not sure what state he will be in if he does pull through. Apparently he received some massive blows to the head, and the doctors are worried that he may remain in a vegetative state even if he does pull through.'

'How terrible,' said Hewitt.

'I've told Dalton to remain at the hospital for now, but I plan to send another female officer over this evening to take over from her and to stay with Mrs Marsh through the night.'

'That's good,' replied Hewitt. 'Please keep me informed on his progress.'

'I will, sir,' Carmichael said as he rose and made his way to the door.

'You and your team did a great job on this one, Steve,' said Hewitt. 'It's just a shame that so many people had to die before we caught him.'

Carmichael nodded gently. 'I only wish we had realised sooner that the body we found in Monroe's house was that of his brother, and if Lillia had written in English in her diary that would have helped too.'

'I fully agree,' replied Hewitt as Carmichael reached the door, 'but you were successful in apprehending the killer and have a full confession in less than two weeks from him committing the first murder. You should not be so hard on yourself. I know that does not help the other poor victims and their families, but at least it's now all over.'

'It's not over yet for Allison Marsh and her girls,' muttered Carmichael as he slowly walked out of Hewitt's office.

To her delight Sam Crouch had managed to get the weekend off so she could go and spend some time in Huddersfield with Bartholomew Green. Knowing this would mean she could not attend Penny's surprise anniversary party on the Saturday, Sam felt it was only good manners to tell Penny in person.

When Sam arrived at Penny's house Steve had not yet returned home; in fact only Penny and Jemma were in the house.

'Oh, hi Sam,' said Penny as she opened the door. 'Come in.'

Penny took Sam through to the kitchen where she and Jemma had been working out who was coming to the surprise party that Saturday. 'I'm going to have to call them and get a few more places booked,' said Penny. 'I reserved twenty seats, but it looks like we will have at least twenty-four, and now Jemma has just advised me she has a new boyfriend she would like to bring too.'

'Oh,' said Sam, looking straight at Jemma. 'Who's the lucky lad?'

Jemma tried to sound very calm. 'It's a boy I know from school. You wouldn't know him, his name's Mike.'

'His name's Mike Hornby,' interrupted Penny. 'I've not met him yet.'

'That would be Mrs Hornby's son,' replied Sam. 'She was the lady who came into the salon the other day when you were there, Penny.' Penny tried to recall the person, but she had not paid too much attention and her recollection of the lady was not good.

'She was wearing a lovely diamond and gold necklace that Mike had bought her for her birthday last week,' commented Sam. 'It was very striking and looked very expensive. I'd say that this Mike is a nice thoughtful lad. You should keep hold of him.'

Jemma was pleased that Sam had given her new boyfriend a vote of confidence as she desperately wanted her Mum and Dad to like him.

'Actually,' continued Sam, 'wasn't it Mike who found the body in the lake the other week?'

'Yes,' confirmed Jemma, 'that was Mike.'

'Really?' replied Penny. 'You never said. So your Dad will already know him.'

'Fortunately not,' Jemma exclaimed. 'He said that he was interviewed by a pretty young woman. I think it must have been Rachel Dalton. He won't have met Dad.'

'Anyway,' said Sam with a slight sign of nervousness. 'I came to tell you that I'm not going to be able to make it on Saturday after all.'

'Why?' exclaimed Penny.

'Because I'm going over to Yorkshire to spend the weekend with Bart,' replied Sam.

'I'm sorry, but I know you'll understand.'

Penny smiled. 'Yes of course I do,' she said. 'At least that means we may only need a few more places.'

Rachel was still at the hospital, but Cooper and Watson were both at their desks when Steve arrived back in the office. 'The Chief has praised us on a job well done,' he said, although his monotone delivery did not suggest he himself shared Hewitt's view.

Cooper forced a smile. 'Well, at least we now know who the killer was and we know for sure that it's over.'

'You're right,' concurred Carmichael.

'And we have also cleared up all the burglaries,' said Watson. 'And in so doing given the local and national press something to talk about.'

Carmichael laughed. 'Yes, that was a great result.'

'Did you see the headlines in today's *Sun?*' said Watson with a grin as he held up the paper.

Hello hello hello ...Village Burglar is Special Constable.

'Oh my God,' exclaimed Carmichael as he

grabbed the paper. 'I expect this will be a major embarrassment to the powers that be.' Steve took a few moments to read through the copy, before returning it to the table in front of him.

'Let's call it a day, guys,' he said. 'We can do a de-brief in the morning when Rachel is here. You've all worked really hard for the last couple of weeks, so get yourselves home and get some rest.'

Cooper and Watson did not need to be told a second time. Within five minutes they had gathered up their things and were away for the evening. Steve remained for a few minutes longer before taking his leave. On the way out he took down a picture of Lillia Monroe that had been fastened to the main board in the office. It was the picture that he had seen for the first time in her office. He shook his head gently as he looked at the face of the pretty young woman in a red dress that stared back at him. 'It's all over now,' he said before placing the photograph in his pocket.

That evening the Carmichael family celebrated Robbie's GCSE results with a Chinese takeaway. With both Jemma and Robbie now happy with their results, the at-

mosphere in the house was much more relaxed.

Steve lifted up a glass of beer and toasted
his son. 'Here's to you, Robbie.'

'And to you too Jemma for getting good
results at A level,' added Penny.

For the first time in weeks Robbie smiled
before gulping back the glass of beer that his
dad had conceded he could have as it was a
special occasion.

It was not until late that evening, when the
children had retired to their rooms, that
Penny brought up the case. As they sat next
to each other on the sofa, Penny wrapped
her arm around Steve's neck. 'So, how did it
go today?' she asked.

'It's just about closed,' said Steve quietly.
'We caught the killer, it was her husband
after all.'

'You said you thought it was him,' Penny
reminded him.

'Yes,' said Steve with more than a hint of
sarcasm, 'and if it wasn't for the fact that he
had a cast iron alibi and then we thought he
was murdered, he was always my main suspect.'

Steve pulled out the photograph of Lillia
and held it in front of him. 'What a waste,'
he sighed. 'She was clearly a bit of a madam,

but she did not deserve to die like she did, and for what?'

Penny took the photograph from her husband. 'Did you ever find the necklace she was wearing?' she asked.

'No,' replied Steve. 'I suspect she was wearing it the day she died, but I imagine it's now lying at the bottom of the lake.'

Penny's thoughts went back to the conversation she had had with Sam Crouch earlier that day. 'I suspect you are right,' she said although she was pretty sure she knew where she could find it.

Chapter 34

Saturday 25th August was Steve and Penny Carmichael's wedding anniversary. Normally for several weeks leading up to this date, Penny would drop heavy hints about what she would like to do to celebrate the occasion, but this year she had not said a word, and with all the time he had been spending on the Lillia Monroe case, Steve had not even had time to get her a card until the evening before. To his amazement though,

Penny seemed totally relaxed when he only gave her a card that morning. He was surprised again when, after he suggested that maybe they went out for a meal somewhere, Penny merely said she would think about it. And totally flabbergasted when Penny said that she would be quite happy to just stay in that evening.

It was almost lunchtime when Penny eventually said they should go out that night, but even then she was adamant that he should not book anything, as they could just pop into a pub somewhere in one of the outlying villages. This sounded perfect to Steve.

That afternoon, as Steve was pottering around, Penny decided she needed to pay an unannounced call on her daughter's new boyfriend. Given that the boy was shortly going to be introduced to her husband, she felt she needed to act quickly. There was only one family called Hornby in the Moulton Bank telephone directory, so it had not taken a great deal of skill for her to locate Michael Hornby's house. It was easy for Penny to make an excuse to get out of the house.

'We've run out of washing powder,' she had shouted up the stairs in the direction of

Steve's office. 'I'm just popping out for a few moments to get some.'

After receiving a muted 'OK' from upon high Penny quickly grabbed her car keys and went out of the front door.

Janet Hornby was a widow, who had brought up her only son Michael on her own following the death of her husband ten years earlier. She was a decent woman, who had worked hard at a variety of badly paid part-time jobs to make ends meet. She idolised Michael, who was her only son and who reminded her so much of the loving husband who had died so suddenly all those years before.

When Penny rang the doorbell it was Janet who answered the door.

'Hello,' Janet said meekly. 'Can I help you?'

Penny introduced herself as the mother of Michael's new girlfriend, a rather strange thing to be doing, she thought, but this was enough to gain her entry into the Hornby house.

It took Penny no more than twenty minutes to conclude her discussions with Janet and Michael Hornby. She left the house with a smile of satisfaction on her face and a necklace gently wrapped in tissue paper in her pocket.

Steve had watched Penny drive away. He was glad that she did not want to make a big thing this year of their anniversary. 'After all,' he said to himself, 'it's only nineteen years so it's not a landmark anniversary.'

As soon as his wife's car had disappeared out of sight Steve picked up his mobile and dialled Rachel Dalton. The phone rang several times before it clicked into voice-mail. 'Hello, this is Rachel Dalton,' said the recording. 'I'm not available to take your call but if you care to leave a message I'll call you back as soon as I can.'

'Hello, Rachel, it's Carmichael here,' said Steve in his most authoritative voice. 'If you get a chance can you call me with an update on how Ralf Marsh is doing.' Steve ended the call and wandered downstairs.

Rachel's mobile was next to her on the bedside cabinet when it rang, but she had no intention of allowing it to interrupt the relaxing lie-in she was enjoying with Gregor in his cramped but cosy bedsit.

'I thought we were seeing him this evening?' Gregor said after the message from Carmichael had ended. 'Can he not wait until then?'

'Yes, we are seeing him tonight,' replied Rachel sleepily, 'but it's a surprise that his wife has arranged. He knows nothing about it.'

When Penny arrived home she picked up the post from the hall floor and walked through into the kitchen. Steve was sitting at the table reading the newspaper.

'Hi,' said Penny cheerily as she carefully placed the mail on the table.

Steve looked up from his paper. 'We're popular today,' he said seeing the number of letters they had received.

'Well, it's not every day you celebrate your twentieth wedding anniversary,' she said as she planted a big kiss on her husband's forehead.

As instructed, all the guests who had been invited by Penny to join their anniversary celebration at the White City Stadium were in the private function room at 7 pm. Everyone who had confirmed they would attend was there, with the only exception being her eldest daughter's new boyfriend, who had texted Jemma out of the blue that afternoon to say that he no longer wanted to go out with her.

After he had realised that it was their twentieth wedding anniversary, Steve had become very suspicious. It did not make sense to him for Penny to be so content to just have a low key dinner for two to celebrate such an occasion. He played along though, as he expected his wife would have something up her sleeve and did not want to do anything to compound the fact that he had forgotten it was their twentieth, by spoiling what he fully expected would be a well-planned event of some sort.

It was only after they left home that evening that Penny suggested to Steve they went to the greyhound track for a meal. Steve twigged that it must be a surprise party pretty much straight away, but decided it would be sensible to just play along.

'Surprise!' shouted everyone as Penny and Steve walked into the function room.

Although not totally surprised, Steve was shocked by the number of people that Penny had invited, which included Robbie Robertson, Katie, Barney Green, Marc and Susan Watson, Paul Cooper and his wife (whose name Steve always forgot), Rachel Dalton with her new boyfriend, Hannah De Vere and Stan Foster. Jemma, Robbie and Natalie were also there, with a few friends to keep them company.

'Happy anniversary,' Penny said before giving him a huge kiss. 'Did you have any inkling?'

Steve laughed and was clearly delighted to see so many people there.

'I had no idea until around lunchtime, when it started to dawn on me that you may be up to something as you were being so relaxed about everything,' he said.

'That would be about when you realised it was actually our twentieth anniversary, I suspect,' teased Penny.

'About that time,' Steve conceded.

For the first hour Steve mingled with the guests and to Penny's joy did not once mention the Lillia Monroe murder case. It was only when he spent some time with Hannah De Vere that the conversation meandered in that direction.

'Is everything now concluded with Lillia's murder?' Hannah asked.

'Pretty much,' replied Steve, who was still not sure how Hannah would be with him, given that her husband would almost certainly face a heavy fine or even a short time in prison due to Steve's investigation.

'I understand it was her husband who

murdered her?' said Hannah.

'Yes,' replied Steve. 'Lillia, two others and maybe one more too.'

'Shocking,' replied Hannah. 'It's such a waste.'

'So what will you do now?' Steve asked.

'Do you mean about Charles?' Hannah said.

'Yes,' replied Steve.

'Oh, that's now officially over,' said Hannah with no emotion. 'We will be getting a divorce and Stan and I are planning to try and buy him out of the manor.'

'Really,' said Steve with genuine surprise. 'So you will stay on there?'

'Oh yes,' responded Hannah as if this was never in any doubt. 'If we can manage it we will take the place over. Charles needs the money and Stan and I want to share our lives together, so it seems such a logical thing for him to move out with some cash and for Stan and I to set up home there. If all works out well we will move the kennels there too.'

Steve nodded his approval. 'Well, I hope it all works out well for you both,' he said before moving off to place a bet on the next race.

'Actually,' said Hannah. 'There was one

thing I wanted to ask you.'

'What was that?' Steve enquired.

'Lillia's necklace,' she said. 'Do you know who that will be left to?'

'I've no idea,' said Steve, who was amazed that Hannah was so interested in it.

'Well, could you let me know if you do find out?' she continued. 'It is something I always thought was so beautiful, and I would very much like to buy it from whoever she left it to.'

Steve shrugged his shoulders. 'To be frank with you, Hannah, I have absolutely no idea whether Lillia even left a will and regrettably the necklace has not yet been found. I think it's probably at the bottom of the lake now.'

'I see,' said Hannah, who then smiled serenely and walked away to find Stan.

As Steve watched her walk away he was joined by Rachel Dalton and Gregor.

'I'd like to introduce you to Gregor Padav,' Rachel said. 'He is the man who translated Lillia's diary for us.'

'Pleased to meet you,' said Steve as he shook Gregor's hand. 'I hope you are having a good evening.'

'Very much so,' said Gregor. 'I am having a fantastic time.'

'I got your message, sir,' interrupted Rachel. 'There is no real change with Mr Marsh, I'm afraid. He's still on a life-support machine and it's not looking good.'

Steve nodded. 'It would appear he got his comeuppance after all,' he said, referring to the conversation he had with Rachel on the first occasion they had visited his home, exactly a week earlier.

'Yes,' Rachel said guiltily. 'I feel really bad about what I said that day.'

Steve smiled. 'As I recall I was a bit uncomplimentary myself,' he said. 'I suspect whatever happens now with him – and we all hope he pulls through – his womanising days are now behind him.' With that Steve walked away to find his wife.

Penny was thoroughly enjoying the evening. With the exception of Jemma, who had a face like a busted wellie ever since she received the text from Mike Hornby, all of the guests seemed to be happy and Penny could see that Steve was having a fantastic time.

'This is great,' said Steve as he put his arm around her. 'Have you won much?'

Penny shook her head. 'Actually I've not bet on any races yet.'

'What!' exclaimed Steve. 'If I had your

luck I'd be betting on every one.'

Penny laughed. 'No, I've not had time. I've been talking with our guests.'

'I see,' said Steve. 'And what's the gossip then?'

Penny gave her husband a look of disapproval. 'I had a good chat with Susan Watson, then I spoke with Rachel and that handsome boyfriend of hers and I've just been talking with Katie Robertson.'

'So, nothing to report then?' Steve said in jest.

'Well, nothing you would be interested in, but Katie did say that she and Barney are arranging to go away for a few days in a week or so to the Lakes.'

'That's nice,' replied Steve, who was not that interested.

'But the thing is they are going with Sam Crouch and Bartholomew too,' she said in amazement. 'According to Katie, she and Sam are getting on great now that they both seem to be happily dating their own respective Reverend Greens.'

Steve laughed. 'Just so long as they remember which room to go to in the middle of the night,' he said. 'Believe me, if you get them mixed up it can prove to be very confusing.'

Penny looked at him in horror. 'I doubt that there will be any goings on of that nature,' she said indignantly. 'After all, they are both men of the cloth.'

Steve shook his head. 'Sometimes you can be so naive,' he said.

It was after midnight when the taxi containing the Carmichael family arrived at their house. Steve had elected to have a few drinks so had left his car at the stadium, which he decided he would go back to collect the following day.

Jemma, who appeared to have quickly got over the breakup with Mike Hornby, Robbie, who was clearly a little worse for wear after drinking a few too many lagers, and Natalie, who was exhausted, all went to their rooms straight away. Steve and Penny lingered a little longer on the lounge sofa.

'What a brilliant evening,' Steve said. 'You are always full of surprises.'

'I try my best,' replied Penny, who was delighted that the evening had gone so well.

'It was fantastic,' he said. 'I especially liked the "Steve and Penny Carmichael Twentieth Anniversary stakes". How did you manage to arrange that?'

'Easy,' replied Penny, with a look of smug

satisfaction. 'It's not what you know...'

Steve smiled. 'I felt a right prat though when I had to go and present the trophy.'

'I bet you did,' laughed Penny. 'Especially when Marc Watson shouted out, "Make sure you tickle the right end" at you.'

'Yes,' replied Steve. 'I will have to talk to him about that on Monday.'

Penny snuggled up close to Steve.

'Did you speak with Hannah much?' Steve asked.

'No, not really,' replied Penny.

'She was saying that she plans to divorce Charles and try and set up house with Stan at the manor,' said Steve.

'Really?' exclaimed Penny. 'To be honest, she is well shot of that creep and although it's his family estate she is more the lady than he is the lord, I'd say.'

Steve laughed, 'Yes, for sure.'

'I hope she manages to pull it off,' continued Penny. 'I think Stan Foster is quite well off, so let's hope they can do it.'

'The other thing she mentioned,' said Steve, 'was that she would like to own Lillia's necklace, you know the Russian Orthodox cross.' Penny tensed up as she heard her husband mention the cross.

'I told her that we thought it was at the

bottom of the lake,' he said, 'and anyway, we don't think Lillia left a will.'

Penny tried hard to appear to be un-interested but could not help asking her husband a further question. 'If it did turn up, who would be entitled to it if there was no will?'

Steve thought for a moment. 'Lillia's nearest living relatives, I suppose,' he said, 'and if they cannot be traced it would be sold off and the proceeds would go to the government.'

'Really,' exclaimed Penny. 'That seems a bit unfair.'

'It makes no odds,' said Steve with a yawn. 'It's not going to turn up now.'

Chapter 35

'You did what?' exclaimed Sam Crouch when Penny recounted the details of her meeting with Janet and Michael Hornby at the salon the following week. 'I don't believe you.'

'What else was I to do?' replied Penny. 'I couldn't let her go around wearing it, and if

I had told Steve he would have been compelled to investigate it and would have almost certainly had to arrest Jemma's new boyfriend. Can you imagine how that would have gone down with Jemma? Anyway, I'm glad I did as Mrs Hornby was such a nice person who has clearly worked hard bringing up her son alone and, apart from this one lapse on his part, it looks like she has done a great job as far as I can see.'

Sam looked bemused. 'I would say that stealing an expensive necklace off a dead body is more than a little lapse,' she said.

Penny thought for a moment. 'Yes, I agree it is quite serious, but anyway the outcome is that the necklace has been returned, nobody is being punished, Mrs Hornby still has her son and Steve, when he gets it, will be none the wiser.'

'So Steve has not received the necklace yet?' Sam queried with a look of complete incredulity.

'No,' replied Penny sheepishly. 'I am going to post it to the station this afternoon.'

Sam shook her head in disbelief, 'And of course the romance between Jemma and Mike has ended.'

'Actually,' said Penny. 'That was not a condition of the deal I did with them. I suspect that was Mrs Hornby's doing.'

Sam nodded. 'Either that, or more likely young Mike was embarrassed at the thought of having to meet you again knowing that you knew he was a thief.'

Penny had not thought about that, but had to concede that it was probably what had happened.

'Anyway, I think Jemma is well shot of him,' Sam said, 'and I'd say that he's bloody lucky you didn't just turn him in.'

It was a further three days before Penny finally plucked up the courage to post the small Jiffy bag containing Lillia's necklace to her husband at Kirkwood police station.

Chapter 36

(4 weeks later)

After many weeks of heart searching, Allison Marsh finally decided that the hospital could turn off her husband's life-support machine. Ralf was effectively brain dead and the doctors had told her he was not going to regain consciousness. On hearing this news Carmichael decided it would be only good manners for him to pay Mrs Marsh a visit and express his personal condolences.

As his car pulled up on the gravel drive, Steve could hear the children playing in the garden. He slowly walked up to the front door and rang the bell. To his surprise the door was opened by a young blonde woman who Steve quickly assessed to be in her late teens or early twenties.

'Is Mrs Marsh at home?' he enquired, holding up his identity card.

The young woman shook her head. 'No, Mrs Marsh is at work,' she replied in a strong eastern European accent.

'At work,' said Steve, who had not anticipated this reply. 'Where does she work?'

The young woman mulled over the question for a few seconds before replying. 'She is at her office.'

Steve puffed out his cheeks. 'And that would be where?' he probed.

'Gemini,' replied the girl with a degree of amazement. 'She is the Managing Director.'

It was now Steve's turn to look astonished. 'I see,' he said.

He started to walk back towards his car

then turned suddenly to face the blonde girl once more. 'Are you Mrs Marsh's new au pair?' he asked.

'Yes,' she responded with a pretty smile. 'My name is Blanka, I started here last week.'

Steve smiled back at the au pair. 'Nice to meet you, Blanka,' he said as he yanked open the car door.

There were no empty seats in the foyer of Gemini Technologies when Steve arrived. They were all occupied by young, smartly dressed men, who had the nervous look of interview candidates.

'Can I see Mrs Marsh?' Steve asked the young receptionist.

'Are you here for the Finance Manager position?' she asked with a degree of surprise in her voice.

'No,' said Carmichael firmly. 'I'm from the police and would like ten minutes of Mrs Marsh's time if that is possible.'

'I'll see if she can fit you in,' replied the receptionist with a smile. Steve waited patiently for a few minutes until he was greeted by Ruth Andrews, who descended the staircase, grasped Steve's hand and shook it aggressively. 'Nice to see you again, Inspector,' she said. 'Allison will see you now, if you would care to follow me.'

Steve followed Ruth Andrews up to the next floor, where Lillia Monroe, Tom Sharwood and Ralf Marsh's offices had been. To his amazement their name plates had already been removed from their office doors and on two of the doors new name plates had been put up with the words: Allison Marsh, Managing Director on one and Ruth Andrews, Commercial Manager on the other.

'I see congratulations are in order?' Carmichael said as he saw Ruth's new title.

'Thank you,' she replied with a broad smile. 'Allison has been very generous in asking me to take on such an important role here.'

'Not at all,' said Allison with an equally broad smile as she emerged from her office. 'With your knowledge, experience and drive I would have been an idiot not to offer you the job.'

Carmichael shook Allison Marsh by the hand and followed her into her office. Once he was safely inside Ruth Andrews reminded her new boss that her next interview was with Adam Rushmore in ten minutes. She then excused herself and left, closing the door behind her.

'She is so efficient,' remarked Allison. 'I have no idea what Ralf was thinking of when he appointed Lillia Monroe in that role in front of her.'

Before Steve could answer Allison continued. 'Actually we both do know what the reason was, don't we, Inspector?'

Steve smiled ruefully. 'I was sorry to hear that your husband did not pull through,' he said, trying to be as sincere as he could.

Allison gazed back at him and sighed. 'Thank you, Inspector Carmichael. I really appreciate that.'

'So you are in charge now?' he said.

'Yes,' replied Allison. 'Ralf will be turning in his grave to think that an airhead like me is now running his baby, but it seemed the obvious thing to do. I may prove to be totally useless at it,' she continued, 'but I'm going to give it my best shot, and with Ruth's help and the support of the rest of the people here you never know, I might do him proud.'

'I'm sure you will,' said Steve with genuine feeling.

'And if just one of the young men downstairs has the ability to match their good looks, then we may also find ourselves a decent Finance Manager to complete my management team. Although I can assure you, Inspector, that whatever his talents and however good-looking he is, he won't be joining me at the Lindley Hotel every Wednesday evening. I don't think we'll continue that particular company tradition now Gemini is under new management.'

Steve smiled but was not sure how to follow that particular comment.

'I've always been more attracted to older and more dominant men myself,' said Allison, with a devilish glint in her eye. 'Men in power like your good self are much more my type.'

The bluntness of her comments surprised Steve. It was certainly at odds with the impression she had given him on their previous meetings. It also made him feel slightly uncomfortable, particularly as he could not work out whether she was just joking with him or genuinely trying to make a play for him.

'I met Blanka at the house,' he said in an attempt to change the subject. 'Where is she from?' he asked.

'Poland,' replied Allison. 'She's very new to us but the girls love her so it's so far so good.'

'Well,' said Carmichael. 'I just wanted to

pay my respects to you and to say that if there is anything that I can do to help you then please let me know.'

'Thank you,' replied Allison, with a wry smile. 'I'm sure to take you up on that, Inspector.'

Feeling decidedly uneasy, Carmichael stood up and went to shake hands with the new MD of Gemini Technologies. Ignoring his outstretched hand, Allison leaned forward and placed a large kiss on Steve's right cheek.

'I hope to see you again very soon,' she said and the way she said it and the look she had in her eye as she spoke, left Steve in no doubt that she meant every word.

That night as Steve lay silently in bed, listening to the gentle snoring emanating from the women beside him, his mind drifted back to the Lillia Monroe case. Having had a few weeks to let the dust settle he was now pleased with the team's results and was no longer frustrated at not cracking the case sooner. However, there were three things that continued to baffle him. Firstly, he wondered how someone as young as Lillia could have the ability to captivate so many men and manipulate them so easily, and secondly, he speculated long and hard, but with no success, about who had sent him Lillia's necklace. The third thing that amazed him was just how easily Allison Marsh appeared to have got over the death of her husband and how forward she had been with him that afternoon. He had to admit that he had been attracted to her from the first time he saw her, but the way she had teased him that morning had caught him way off guard. As he contemplated her words and the way she had flirted with him, his mind started to ramble away to thoughts of an illicit affair with the new widow Marsh and the sweet pleasure that might bring him. However, these thoughts did not last for too long as, despite her heavy breathing, Steve loved Penny dearly and he quickly dispelled any thoughts of the widow Marsh from his mind.

He gently rolled over to face his wife, who still remained as beautiful to him now as the day he first saw her. He placed his arm around her soft waist.

'So, you still love me then,' she murmured.

'Of course I do,' he whispered in her ear. 'But I do wish you didn't snore so loudly.'

Penny turned to face him. She slowly

opened one eye which fixed him in it's fierce glare. 'How many times do I have to tell you,' she told him, 'I don't snore!'

The publishers hope that this book has given you enjoyable reading. Large Print Books are especially designed to be as easy to see and hold as possible. If you wish a complete list of our books please ask at your local library or write directly to:

Magna Large Print Books
Magna House, Long Preston,
Skipton, North Yorkshire.
BD23 4ND

This Large Print Book, for people
who cannot read normal print,
is published under the auspices of

THE ULVERSCROFT FOUNDATION